INCARCERATED SCARFACES

A life sentence is usually the end of the road for an inmate. All that lies ahead is years of appeals, details, and danger. The biggest past time for incarcerated men and women is trying to find activities to pass the time.

Some can spend hours a day reading or watching TV. Others play sports or board games to relieve the boredom. While some others write letters, poems, journals, and novels.

Incarcerated Scarfaces is a collection of writings from four Georgia inmates.

It's unapologetically street lit, but you could just learn a lesson.

Volume 1 includes stories by best selling urban-lit authors Sa'id Salaam, Hood Chronicles, Billie Miff, and newcomer Deshion Hightower.

Incarcerated Scarfaces gives these men an outlet to tell their stories as well as help themselves. The royalties go directly to the authors to relieve the burdens on family and friends. Helping with ongoing legal fees as well as commissary and the etceteras that are necessities.

URBAN AESOP PRESENTS

INCARCERATED SCARFACES

AN ANTHOLOGY FEATURING

SA'ID SALAAM   **HOOD CHRONICLES**   **KATAVIOUS ELLIS**   **ADAM UPPERMAN**

Urban Aesop Presents

INCARCERATED SCARFACES

An Anthology Featuring
Sa'id Salaam
Hood Chronicles
Deshion Hightower
Billie Miff

Said Salaam

Sa'id Salaam hails from the Bronx, New York. He recalls wanting to be an author from an early age. His love of literature stemmed from his mother reading bedtime stories to him as a child.

He didn't pen his first story until becoming incarcerated on trumped up charges of murder. He maintains his innocence and is aggressively fighting the wrongful conviction. Meanwhile, he puts the pen to the paper at an incredible rate.

To date, Sa'id has written and published over sixty titles from a prison cell. A student of the industry, he decided to self publish and started his own publishing company. Urban Aesop Publications has a growing roster of some of the best new authors in the game. He initially started the company out of necessity after a bad deal with a shady publisher. It also allows him to help other incarcerated authors get their stories out to the world.

Sa'id is widely regarded as one of the freshest voices in the game. His diverse catalog shows why. He is well known for his vivid descriptions, hilarious wit, and dynamic wordplay. Fans call him the Aesop of urban lit because of the real life lessons he weaves into his stories. He was once called the "next Donald Goines" to which he replied, "Thanks, but no thanks. I'm the first Sa'id Salaam." While clearly honored by the accolade, he relishes his individuality and blazes his own path.

His books are available in e-book, audio, as well as paperback. Check him out on Amazon, retail bookstores, and even your local library.

Read more about Sa'id Salaam in the June 2015 issues of *Don Diva* and *Gorilla Convict*. Be sure to *like* the Free Sa'id Salaam page and visit him at Saidsalaam.com

Some of Sa'id Salaam titles include:

Love and Hip Hop
Ra and Dre
Dope Boy
Dope Girl
Reverend Cash
Killa
Yolo
Family Drama
Luv in the Club
Rotten Lil Peaches
Bad Cop
The Last 48
and many more...

Acknowledgements

All praise and thanks is for Allah the lord of everything in existence.

In sha Allah I wrote this book for the entertainment of my Muslim brothers and sisters as well as those faithful readers who enjoy my other books.

Islam, worshipping Allah in the manner sent down in the Qur'an and Sunnah are paramount in my life. I pray this reflects it.

Any good contained in it is from Allah. Anywhere I may have erred is from myself. May the peace and blessing of Allah be on us all.

BLACK INK PUBLICATIONS PRESENTS

THE LAST [48]

SA'ID SALAAM

The Last 48
A Short Story by
Sa'id Salaam

7:00 AM Friday

"Hmph!" Marlo fussed as she looked at herself in the full-length mirror. The 38-year-old woman could easily pass for ten years younger. It had been twenty years since she'd given birth to her one and only child and that was plenty of time to get her body back tight and right, just like it was.

It wasn't vanity that made her huff indignantly— it was the date. Today was her son Thad's twentieth birthday. It was also the day his killer was due to be released from prison.

"Two years for killing my child. Seven hundred and twenty days for taking my Thaddeus away from me," she said for the seven hundred and twentieth time. Not a day had gone by that she didn't mourn the loss of her only child or curse his killer.

The part that made it even worse was that she actually knew his killer. She'd practically raised him since he lived right across the street in her southwest Atlanta neighborhood.

She'd helped raise Carlos aka Lil' Los since his mother, Nita, hadn't been that interested in being a mother. However, she did know all of the latest dances and could roll a blunt like nobody's business. She just sucked at parenting. Physically, Nita was a year older than Marlo, but mentally, she was twenty years her junior. In another dose of insult to injury, the woman had been turning her nose up at her since the "incident". That's what they called her son's murder since Carlos claimed it was an accident. Several friends who'd witnessed or heard about it after the fact said the two close friends had fallen out over a-sixteen-year-old named Dana.

Marlo knew the girl was trouble since the first time she saw the half-naked teen prancing around the neighborhood. Back then, she sure hoped she would have picked Carlos over Thad, but found the girl at her house daily. Several times she'd came home from work to the smell of sex hovering in the air and the two looking guilty. She'd also seen how flirtatious the girl was with other men, including her own.

Back then, she was dating a fellow school teacher named William. He was definitely marriage material, but the stress of her losing her child pushed him away. Marlo was slapped in the face yet again when Dana popped up knocked up shortly after Thad died. She'd claimed from day one that the child was Thad's since he was her first. Carlos was her second and she counted at least three more before the girl had started showing and a few more once she'd given birth to her grandson. Once Thad and Carlos were gone, she was circulated throughout the hood like a STD.

Marlo verified paternity the first chance she got by offering to watch the baby. The young girl wanted to turn up, so she always needed someone to watch him. Marlo watched him in the car seat as she drove straight to a DNA lab. It confirmed what she could tell just by looking at the infant. She was now the proud grandmother of a child whose name she could not pronounce from a young woman she could not stand.

She almost wondered what her Thaddeus saw in the hoochie since she wasn't particularly pretty. Her skin was pockmarked and her wisp of hair was usually gelled down to her scalp. She didn't wear many clothes and it was obvious as to why when she heard the girl was slinging coochie around like a Frisbee. According to people with knowledge, she'd driven a wedge between the close friends when Thaddeus dumped her.

Thad dropped her and found a more suitable girlfriend. One who wore whole shorts and shirts and had a whole future with a whole scholarship. The hood rat didn't like being snubbed, so she started talking to Carlos to spite him. During pillow talk, she said Thaddeus was talking shit about Carlos. Talking shit is a capital offense in the hood because he was dead a day later.

Two days later, Carlos was arrested. Meanwhile, Dana just moved on to the next man. Another friend of her sons who told her that Carlos bragged about intentionally killing her son. The hearsay was inadmissible in court. Plus, he refused to testify. That too was a capital offense that got your ass gunned down in southwest Atl or any hood for that matter.

The prosecutor pointed out the fact that Thad was no saint. He was no demon either, but had once caught a petty weed and possession of gun charge. Another cruel twist since it was Carlos's gun, but Thaddeus took *the charge that would have sent his friend to prison. A good defense lawyer could have taken the arrest and run with it. He'd offered the plea deal rather than take the risk of letting him get off Scott free. Marlo reluctantly agreed, mainly because she literally could not bear to see the person who killed her son every day. With him living directly across the street, she would been forced to.*

Forced to see him laughing and smiling while her son decayed in a box six feet under the earth. Then that nasty little Dana was over there with him. Probably having her grandson over there too, breathing loud packs and listening to loud music.

"Oh God!" Marlo wailed and felt her knees buckle. Luckily, a strong pair of hands caught her and held her up. Just like they'd done when she'd almost collapsed in the courtroom.

"Whoa," Deputy John Jenkins said when he swooped in and caught her. He had been the bailiff in the court when Carlos took his plea. They made eye contact a few times during the process, but it wasn't the time or place for a love connection.

William had just left her citing he couldn't deal with her depression. He'd gotten ghost and left her to deal with it on her own. John had caught her before she hit the floor now just like he did then. Carlos's was the last case of the day, so he'd ended up driving her home. The act of chivalry led to a sex act on the sofa. A furious bout of sex with torn hosiery and panties pulled aside. The pleasure eased her pain for as long as he was inside of her. Somehow, they kept it going two years later. She was in a lot of pain. The peace officer made her feel good and safe by laying plenty of pipe and giving her a pistol to protect herself. A dainty little nine millimeter that packed enough power to kill.

"You know what today is?" she moaned and sank into his embrace.

"Mmhm," he hummed because he didn't. He was going to guess birthday but wasn't quite sure. Perhaps they'd reached some sort of anniversary, but he wasn't as committed as she was. She may have been in a relationship with him, but he still liked to spread love and dick throughout the city.

"*Today is the day that boy comes home. Two years and he's home free while Thaddeus is still gone and ain't never coming back!*" *she wailed.* "*How am I supposed to look at that boy every damn day? Huh?*"

"*Just ignore him. Don't say nothing to him. Don't look at him. You have to get over it,*" *he suggested with a frustrated sigh. He just knew he could get a little action before going on duty. Her tears said otherwise, so he'd have to get off during his shift.*

"*Then—then if it was really a so-called 'accident', then why he ain't never said sorry? Ain't you supposed to be sorry when you have an accident?*" *she pleaded.*

"*Yeah,*" *he said dryly, hoping it was over since they both had work. There would be no sex, so he looked at his watch and announced the time.*

8:15 AM

Deputy Jenkins was now assigned to a car since he got in trouble working in the courthouse. His dick slinging ways got him caught on camera getting a blowjob by a civilian. Being back in a vehicle suit him just fine since he got to be in contact with female fugitives.

"*You go to jail or suck a dick and go home?*" *he laughed, practicing his favorite line. It worked at least once a day, sometimes twice. His record was three but today's lineup looked even more promising. A bad check and credit card ring had been discovered and warrants had been issued.*

Jenkins followed his GPS to a west side apartment complex and parked in front of a unit. He tried to sound out the multiple syllable name, but it was a mouthful. Ghetto enough to hopefully give her a mouthful. A few young dealers scrambled when they saw the uniform. Deputies seldom make drug arrest but they weren't taking any chances.

A skinny dopefiend saw the cop and made beeline in his direction. She knew on duty cops were the biggest tricks so she made her pitch.

"*Tryna get yo dick sucked-ed?*" *she asked with a wink and an extra ed.*

"*Sure am,*" *he laughed and rang the doorbell. The crack addict sucked her yellow teeth and slinked away.*

"Who!" a deep voice boomed from behind the door. The cop unhooked his gun holster as the heavy footsteps came closer. Serving warrants can be extremely dangerous because no one likes to go to jail. The door was snatched open by a four hundred pound woman holding a pound cake in her hand.

"Shanateriza Jackson?" he barked, coming pretty close to nailing the name on the first try. It was close enough that she didn't correct him.

"Huh?" she nodded, identifying herself. She glanced around the living room full of merchandise stolen with stolen credit cards and bad checks.

"I have a warrant for your arrest. Who else is in the house?" he asked, walking in on her. She had no choice but to back up so he could enter.

"Nobody," she pouted, sticking her lip out. The cop looked her up and down, undeterred by her large size.

"Well, you have two choices. You can go to jail or suck some dick?" he explained. Ten minutes later, he emerged from the apartment feeling relaxed and slightly sleepy. "One down, three more to go for the record."

9:00 AM

"Hey, Marlo girl!" Marlo's coworker Janice greeted as she entered the teachers' lounge. She was bubbly from today being Friday and two days away from these bad ass kids.

"Hey, girl," Marlo replied with a sigh and sipped her coffee. Her watched beeped, signaling she was due in class but couldn't find the strength to get up.

"Girl, what's wrong with you! That cop had you up all night, hand-cuffed to your headboard?" she laughed.

"Naw," Marlo said, shaking her head. Last night was one of the rare nights they didn't have sex. He'd tried, but she was just not in the mood for love or sex.

"Well, let's hang out this weekend. It's been a minute," she offered, hoping to cheer her up from whatever had her down.

"Okay," she sighed even though she had no desire to go anywhere or do anything except curl up and die. In a few hours, Carlos would be a free man.

12:30 PM

"Al Hamdulillah, the brother Hasan finna bounce up out this peace!" Abdul-Hakim cheered as he entered the brother's cell.

"Yeah," Hasan croaked unsurely as he sorted out his belongings. He had amassed quite a bit of food and property since his mother kept his books full. "I'm leaving my books to the brothers."

"We good, akhi. Take them with you so you can continue to study. And remember, first stop..."

"The masjid. I know, akhi," he said. In the couple of years, he'd been in prison he'd seen plenty of brothers go home and revert back to the streets as soon as they hit the streets. Mainly because their first stop wasn't the masjid or mosque as it's also called.

In fact, only three out of ten "chain gang" Muslims actually stay on the path once they're released. That's because three out of ten joined the ranks of the Muslims for reasons other than faith. Faith never entered their heart in the first place. Most were just plain scared and wanted the safety that comes with numbers. Prison is a dangerous place that can turn men into mice or women or make them pretend to be Muslims.

Some know from day one that they're faking, while some don't realize until they get released from the stress that is prison. Then their same vices and bad habits overtake them and they're right back in prison.

"You okay, my brother?" Abdul-Hakim laughed to lighten the moment. He could literally see his temples jump from the conflict within. He'd seen the reality of release shake many men in his many years of incarceration. He remembered when Carlos first came in with that city swag until one of the gangs put the press on him. He quickly came to the Muslims and joined the ranks. In prison, you have to join something and the Muslims were the easiest group to join. They didn't jump you in like the gangs.

"Yeah, I..." he began but was cut off when his name was called. *"Welp, I'm out!"*

"Now stay out! Don't fall off and come back, bruh," the brother said and threw open his arms to embrace him.

"I ain't never coming back! Believe that!" he insisted but didn't say *"In sha Allah".* A Muslim never says anything about something to come without saying *"God willing".* Abdul-Hakim thought about that as he watched his brother leave the dorm, to leave the prison.

"Don't come back!" the officer barked as he processed Hasan out of the prison. He could tell someone cared about the kid since he had a check for a couple hundred dollars from his books. Most prisoners only get the $35 bucks the state gives upon release. It didn't matter if you just did thirty five years, all the state of Georgia had for you was $35 bucks.

"I ain't never coming back!" he shot back once again without saying *"God willing".* He like most inmates hated this mean old officer. They claimed he hated young guys. It was partially true because he hated seeing young black men throwing their youths away in prison. Running around the prison with their pants sagging, ripping and running like it was a joke.

"God willing," the officer added since Christians say 'God willing' as well. *"Just keep that kufi on your head and do what you supposed to do!"*

1:00 PM

Hasan nodded and signed his papers to officially become a free man. He deliberately held his breath so his next one would be as a free man. A van drove him to the bus station for the two-hour ride back to his beloved city of Atlanta. For most of the ride, he quietly recited melodic verses from the Qur'an. Halfway to the city he looked at his reflection in the window. He pulled his kufi off just to check his waves. Somehow, the kufi never made it back onto his head. He was Hasan Muwakil when he boarded that bus but two hours later Lil Los stepped off in Atlanta.

1:38 PM

"Whew!" Deputy Jenkins exclaimed as blowjob number two came to an explosive end. So far, he was batting a thousand since no one wanted to go to jail. Especially on a Friday since there would be no seeing of a judge until Monday. That meant a weekend stuck in the dirty, nasty, dangerous Fulton county jail.

Mmhm," Diamonique huffed sarcastically. She knew she had some all-star head and didn't like being coerced out of it. She did have some fly shit from the hot cards, so she acquiesced and sucked him off. "Told you don't come in my mouth!"

"Yeah, but that would have defeated the purpose," he chuckled. The real joke is that the quick fix only lasted a day or so. The unserved warrants go back into a pile to be served again another day. He could get them again and get his dick sucked again or it could go to another deputy and they were going to jail.

The cop probably needed professional help for his sexual addiction because he could and would do this all day.

"So, I'm good?" the wanted fugitive wanted to know.

"Okay, I guess," he shrugged assuming she meant her oral skills. "Catch you later."

2:15 PM

"There goes my baby!" Nita cheered when Carlos stepped from the bus and looked around. He smiled brightly and braced himself for a strong embrace.

"Hey, mama!" he said and laughed as she hugged all the air from his body. He could smell the weed smoke just below the splash of perfume she'd used to mask it. He looked towards Broad Street knowing the masjid was there. Right there, two blocks away. A custom in Islam is to stop by the mosque and pray when returning from a journey. Not a day went by that some returning Muslim stopped by to practice that ritual, except today that is.

"Look at you! Let's go get you something to eat! Shit, I'm hungry too!" she announced as the munchies kicked in from smoking weed.

"Fish Supreme?" he asked hopefully. In his defense, that's some good ass fish, but he was already abandoning his adopted religion.

"Hell yeah!" she cheered and pulled him to the car where a man waited behind the wheel.

"Sup?" the driver greeted with a head nod as they reached the car.

"Catfish, this my son Carlos. Carlos, this is Catfish," she said, making the formal introduction. As formal as could be with a grown man named after a fish species.

"Sup," he greeted back and winced from the weed smoke hovering on the car's headliner. It had been two years since he smoked, but it was a daily habit before that. He thought about intoxicants being forbidden in Islam when Catfish passed a smoldering blunt into the back seat. He debated for a whole second and a half before accepting it.

"Welcome home, baby!" Nita cheered when her son took a deep pull on the blunt despite him having to check in with probation on Monday morning. Most prisoners who are released on a weekend end up turning up all weekend, then turning up dirty when they get pissed tested on Monday. Parole ends up being a weekend pass for many a drug addicts. Habitual potheads are just as much drug addicts as cocaine and heroin users.

2:45 PM

Catfish pulled into the parking lot of a Fish Supreme near the house. He looked at both mama and son snoring from the strong weed and shook his head. He reached over and groped a titty to wake her up, but it didn't work. Nita had been fucked in her sleep before, so a simple titty squeeze didn't even register.

"Nita! Say, Nita!" he called out while shaking her. The noise and movement woke Carlos instantly. Sudden noises would forever put him on high alert after what he'd experienced in prison.

"What's up?" he asked, leaning forward just as his mother stretched her arms and wiped a line of drool from her chin.

"We finna eat is what's up!" Catfish replied and hopped out. Nita and Carlos got out and followed him inside.

"You ain't shit!" Nita griped when her boyfriend made a separate order and paid for it. "You got money son?"

"I ain't cashed my check yet," he said almost apologetically.

"Don't worry. It's my treat," she sang and dug under her wife beater and into her bra. She produced a ten-dollar bill moist from the heat and sweat of her softball-sized breast.

"Thanks. Let me get a fish supreme, hush puppies and a sweet tea!" he said, rubbing his hands together deviously. His mother shook her head and laughed, then placed the order.

"I'm finna run next door and cash my check," he said since it would be a couple of minutes before the fish came out of the hot grease.

"Grab me a forty. And some scrawberry blunt wraps!" she said, aiming to get back what she was spending on the meal.

"Kay, mama," he said and hit the door. The liquor store shared a space in the same strip mall, so it was a short walk. Again, he was reminded of Islam's prohibition on intoxicants as he dug his mother's favorite malt liquor from a tub of ice. He grabbed another for himself and approached the counter.

"Got ID?" the clerk asked, asking about the check, not the alcohol sale. He would sell liquor to a two year old but wasn't getting stuck on no bad check.

"Uh, yeah," Carlos replied, digging out his prison issue identification card. Ironically, he kept it in his pocket size Qur'an. He ignored the contradiction and handed it over. The clerk held it up to compare faces and nodded.

"How long you did?" he asked, guessing it was nowhere near the ten years he'd once did since the kid was only twenty.

"Two," Carlos said with a proud nod since doing a bid is a badge of honor in the hood. The clerk chuckled at the *"skid bid"* and completed the transaction. He shook his head knowingly at the kid as he walked out. He knew if he was buying alcohol and weed with his *"coming home"* check, he was going back.

"You ain't get me one?" Catfish frowned, seeing he only brought two bottles.

"Nigga, you ain't buy us no food, but you want a free beer! Boy, stop!" Nita fussed on behalf of her son.

"Tryna front in front ya son," he pouted like men raised by their mamas tend to do. They can be downright bitchy and bitch-like at times. They want and expect every woman to cater and coddle them like their mama does.

"Boy, stop," she repeated and patted his hand to comfort him. "I'll let you have some of mine. 'Kay?"

Carlos twisted his lips at the display. He'd always viewed his mother as just a mother but now realized she was a woman. Islam came back to mind and reminded him that men are the protectors and maintainers of women. He failed in that and left his mother to the likes of Catfish. It was cool because he was home now. He dreamed of teaching his mother about Islam and imagined her covering, fasting and praying. Now wasn't a good time, so he would just wait 'til later. Once he had her alone and once the drugs and alcohol wore off.

"You ready, baby?" Nita cooed, snapping him back to the present. Both he and Catfish replied in the affirmative, assuming she meant them.

3:15 PM

"What the—" deputy Jenkins wondered at his next fugitive. The name Raynard Starr was normal enough, but all the aliases raised his eyebrows and curiosity. "Raynisha, Starlleta, Denisha."

He frowned up at the mug shots in different names and genders. He was a handsome man when he wanted to be but also a pretty, pretty girl, as well. A warrant is a warrant, so he shrugged his shoulders and hopped out of the car. He adjusted his utility belt like Batman and walked towards the door.

"Who?" a woman's voice called as the sound of heels click clicking on the tile floors sang backup. The sounds of the lock being unlocked prevented him from replying since he would see who was ringing as soon as he opened the door. "Ooh!"

"Raynard Starr?" he asked, looking the man in full drag up and down. A tank top showed off the brand new breast he bought from cashing hot checks. He looked sexy even though he had a dick under the short skirt he wore.

"He not here. I'm Raynisha," he said, nodding to make the cop believe it.

"That's fine cuz I have a warrant for that name, too," he said, nodding so he would believe him, too. He stepped up and inside, forcing Raynard to step back or get stepped on.

"You really gotta lock me up?" he pleaded in falsetto, batting his false lashes. He saw the way the cop locked in on the manmade breast and did a little shimmy to show them off. This certainly wouldn't be his first cop.

"Bruh, are you trying to seduce me?" Jenkins scoffed indignantly.

"I most certainly am!" he said, turning on his well-rehearsed feminine charm.

3:35 PM

"Three down. One more for the record!" he said when he left the apartment twenty minutes later. A record is a record, so he shrugged his shoulders and got back into his car. He should have driven himself to some rehab for sex addicts. Instead, he drove towards trouble.

Twenty minutes after that, he arrived at yet another fugitive's last known address and got out. The pretty, little, white girl made his dick jump in anticipation. Some white girl head would be the perfect way to close out a record setting day. He still planned to spend a night with Marlo to make up for what he missed last night.

"Yes?" Becky asked and flipped her good hair as she answered the door. She almost expected the police to show up after using what she knew was a stolen card. She was glad her lawyer dad was out with her lawyer mom so they wouldn't find out.

"Rebecca Shaw?" he asked, using his official deputy sheriff voice. As professional as he tried to be, his eyes still scanned her from blonde hair to pink toes.

"Yes?" she demanded, taken aback by the flirtatious gawk. She now wished her lawyer dad and lawyer mom were home. "Can I help you?"

"No, but I might be able to help you. Actually, you can help yourself. I have a warrant for your arrest on charges of bank fraud. I would hate for you to have to spend all weekend in that nasty jail."

"So would I. I need to call my dad!" she whined.

"You'll get a call once you get to the jail," he advised and removed his cuffs. "Unless... you want to work it out?"

"Can I?" she pleaded and opened her mouth to ask how but he reached for his zipper to explain. The girl's tears didn't stop her from doing what she had to do so she could stay free.

Her tears didn't stop the cop from thoroughly enjoying some white girl head. They certainly didn't stop the surveillance cameras from recording the entire incident including the sound. Not just the slurping and moans from the blowjob in progress, but the crime that led up to it as well.

4:35 PM

Carlos let out a lonely sigh when he looked at the mosque as they drove past it on Cascade. He heard the call to prayer and saw the brothers entering, knowing it was time to pray. His mind screamed to Catfish to pull over, so he could go pray but Catfish could barely read text so he certainly couldn't read his mind. When he opened his mouth the taste of beer closed it back. He couldn't pray while inebriated.

"We home!" Nita cheered when the driver barreled into the driveway. The first thing Carlos saw was his old hooptie sitting on cinder blocks. Nita's car was beside it badly in need of being washed. Although not quite as bad as the grass needed to be cut. Proof Catfish didn't do much around the house except the plumbing. He laid plenty of pipe and that was enough for Nita.

"What happened to my rims?" he asked, cocking his head. At one point, he would have killed or died for the huge chrome wheels. Now he was just curious since he planned to sell it and buy something more befitting of a Muslim. Wasting of wealth is a sin in Islam and big chrome rims were definitely a waste. There's nothing wrong with having nice things, but extravagance is frowned upon. After all, spendthrifts are the brother of the devil.

"I'on know," Nita said out her mouth, but the guilt on her face was obvious. During rough times, she sold them to get over the hump. At least she did put some of the money on his books. "Don't even worry 'bout them. I'll buy you some more!"

"A'ight," he said and shrugged since he really didn't care. As soon as he stepped out of the car, his head was magnetically pulled across the street. His heart ached so much, it made his knees buckle causing him to hold on to the car for support.

"That loud pack got 'em!" Catfish cheered since stuff like that was important to him. He could give a fuck about Syria, Dow Jones, or global warming. His chief concern was getting high and getting laid.

"You okay, baby?" Nita asked genuinely concerned. She followed his eyes across the street and sighed. "I know, baby."

The trio made it inside and flopped on the sofa and chair. The beers were cracked open again and another blunt was put in the air. Carlos felt his eyes getting heavy and tried to fight. He was no match against the alcohol and strong weed; especially after being clean and sober for almost two years.

"Come on," Catfish said once he blinked himself to sleep. He was so use to dealing with baby mamas, so he knew the best time to put his dick in them is as soon as the kid goes to sleep.

"Okay," Nita giggled and followed him down to her room. They stripped like it was a race and flopped naked on the bed.

"Suck a nigga dick or something?" he asked romantically.

"Eat a bitch out!" she shot back indignantly. He blew his breath in defeat and climbed on top of her. She reached down and guided him inside. As soon as he was in, he began to hump rhythmically. Meanwhile in the living room, Carlos began to dream.

"I wonder what Thad doing?" Dana asked, stifling a giggle. She loved seeing Carlos get jealous over her. She'd never been loved before, so jealousy would have to do.

"What you asking 'bout him 'fo?" he shot back like she knew he would. Especially since they were naked on his bed making out.

"I was just asking! Dang!" she cooed and reached for his erection. She knew she was pregnant since she hadn't had a period since Thad's rubber broke. She was so smitten, she put her whole hoe tendencies on pause and had no doubt it was his. He hit it a few times and moved on to the next girl. A cute, clean little thing who read books and spoke properly. She just couldn't understand why he chose her over her when she was freaking him any way he wanted it.

"You like this, huh?" Carlos grunted as he humped away inside of her. He was glad she didn't make him wear a condom, so he could feel the heat and liquidity first hand. Why would she since she couldn't get any more pregnant?

"Mmhm," she moaned and wiggled under him. He didn't last long in the young box that still had the elasticity that makes vaginas great. Misuse and abuse can leave one stretched out and useless like an old pair of socks that fall down around the ankles. She gave a kegel squeeze and it was a wrap.

"Argh! Mm, shit!" he cussed and fussed, making crazy faces while pumping her full of semen.

"Mmm, Thaddeus. You got that good love," she moaned and squeezed a little more.

"Bitch, get the fuck up out my shit!" he demanded and snatched out. "Calling me by the next nigga name!"

"No, I didn't?" she whined, enjoying the show. It was all she could do not to laugh in his face at the look on his face. Her simple mother told her if a man won't whoop your ass, he don't love you. She was trying to get him to show her some love.

"Thad told me you was hoe!" he shot back to heap some hurt to match his.

"And he told me you was lame!" she said, reaching for her panties. The remark pouted his lips in disbelief.

"My nigga ain't said nothing like that!" he demanded hotly. As much as he looked up to Thaddeus, he knew he wasn't insulting him to some neighborhood jump off.

"Yeah, he did!" she insisted since she saw she'd hit a nerve. "Said you a lame and yo' mama is a hoe. Said she tried to give him some!"

He sank to his bed from the weight of the insults. He knew Nita was generous with her vagina, but a hoe? His mother did always say how handsome Thad was? And he a lame? He wasn't as tall and muscular as his friend, but lame?

"I'm sorry, baby," she cooed and wrapped her arms around him from behind. Her warm, firm breast made him feel a little better in an instant. "He just jealous cuz he knowed I like you."

"Hmph," he wondered, trying to reconcile her words with reality. He tried to push up on her when she first moved into the hood but she was all over Thaddeus. Most girls did like the handsome athlete over him.

He was so deep in thought, he didn't notice her come around and go down. The undeniable pleasure of a hot mouth killed all rational and reasoning. He leaned back and enjoyed the demonstration, while the seed of hate was sown in his heart.

8:00 PM

"Carlos! Wake up, baby!" Nita called, shaking his leg. He was actually relieved to be awakened from the dream since he knew what was going to happen next. He'd relived it so many times, like the radio playing the same song three times every hour. The dream of that day ruined many a night's sleep. He blinked his eyes when he registered she wasn't alone.

"Yeah, nigga! Get yo' ass up!" Mann laughed, kicking his foot. He was surrounded by Fresh and Hot Rod. The gang was all there except for Thad who would be forever late.

"Sup?" Carlos chuckled, seeing his friends. His watch began to beep to remind him it was once again time for prayer.

"Turn up, my nigga!" Hot Rod demanded, sticking a blunt in his face. He contemplated for a moment and made a decision. He would turn up and party tonight, then tomorrow he would make all his prayers and go to the mosque. Islam gave him peace and dignity instead of the chaos and humiliation of his former life.

"Yeah, my nigga!" Mann cheered when he hit the weed. He passed him a tall can of cheap beer to chase it down with.

"And we finna hit the club!" Fresh added and handed him a couple of name brand bags.

"What?" he asked, seeing Nita looking on happily as he dug in the bags and found clothes and tennis shoes.

"I tole them your sizes!" she said so he would know her contribution.

"Something for yo' pocket," Mann said, handing him a roll of cash. The couple hundred looked like more since it was street money consisting of ones, fives, tens and wrapped by twenties.

"Me too!" Hot Rod said, pressing a bag of bagged crack so he could get his hustle back on like before he left. They meant well and thought they were being helpful in their own ghetto ways.

He accepted the drugs even though he vowed never to go back to the trap. Abdul-Hakim had arranged a job for him with one of the brothers. All he had to do was meet him at the masjid. Most of the brothers had their own businesses or hustles and would gladly give him some work. All he had to do was show up.

Tomorrow, he thought to himself because he didn't want to disappoint his friends. He didn't understand that whenever a person truly intends to change, his old friends become his new enemies. Anything else is like taking a bath and putting dirty clothes back on.

"Um, okay," he acquiesced. He left his mom and friends smoking weed as he went to take a shower. Carlos took the ritual bathing Muslims call a ghuls. Except it's to purify for worship, not the club. Instead, he was off to do everything contrary to Islam like Isis or Al Qaeda. Again, he vowed it would just be one night. After all, he owed his mama and friends for making his short stay in prison as comfortable as a stay in prison can be. As bad as confinement is it's even worse being hungry.

Most people believe what they see in prison movies where the inmates go through the chow line while heaping spoonfuls of hot food is heaped on the tray. The truth of the matter is that Georgia's prisons feed grown men like small children. Worse even since there is no lunch on Friday, Saturday, and Sunday. Dinner chow is called from four to five PM and that's a long time until breakfast again the next morning.

"Just one night. Gonna get up for Fajr in the morning, then hit the masjid," he nodded as he washed. He stepped out, dried, and got fresh in his new clothes. He'd hoped all the weed and alcohol had been consumed by the time he got back but no such luck.

"Let mama blow you a gun!" Nita cheered when her son returned. She put the lit end of the blunt in her mouth and began to blow. It was just like old times when he leaned into the steady stream of smoke and inhaled.

"Yeah, my nigga!" Hot Rod shouted when he began taking it up his nostrils. He took his place when he fell away full of smoke. Nita had enough breath to fill his lungs as well.

"What club y'all finna hit?" Nita asked offhanded, hoping for an invite. Catfish got ghost after he got off so she wouldn't mind hanging out with them. It was either that or the local American Legion and gin with some old player trying to lay his old pipe.

"We finna hit that 231!" Mann cheered, but left out the part about her coming with. Once the weed was depleted, they hit the door to hit the club.

10:00 PM

Marlo heard the laughter outside and got up to investigate. She grabbed her pistol from her purse and went to her front door. The black burglar bars allowed her to stand in her doorway and see without being seen. Her breathing seemed to pause when she saw Carlos smiling from ear to ear. She thought he looked directly at her, although he couldn't see her and laughed heartily. Now her heart stopped as well seeing he thought it was funny.

"My baby is gone and you laughing. It's a joke, huh? A game!" she spat too angry for tears.

"Who you talking to?" John asked as he came out of the bathroom.

"No one," she said and quickly closed the door. He tried to come over but she blocked him with hug and kiss.

"Mmhm," he nodded knowingly at the distraction. If she wanted to offer some sex, he would take it. He kissed her all the way down the hall and into her bedroom.

Marlo quickly stripped and climbed on the bed while John took his time. He marveled down at her firm body and shook his head. Had he been the marrying type he would have married her. Just for her looks alone even though everything else about her was a plus as well. The well-liked, well-respected teacher had dibs on the next assistant princi-pal position that came available. In the meanwhile, she assumed her favorite position on the bed.

John Jenkins was a handsome man but she still preferred not to have to look at him during sex so she put her face down and ass up. She would never admit it, but she really didn't like him. She liked being alone even less so she put up with him.

He came around her and entered her doggy style, like the dog that he was and began to hunch. Luckily, her body responded to the sex act because her mind was a million miles away. Figuratively speaking since it was really just across the street. Her body rocked from the movement but all she saw when she closed her eyes was Carlos's smiling face. It was the same face he'd made when she used to make cookies for them. He would devour the treat, then hug her with all he had. Cookies and love didn't get at home.

"Hmph!" she huffed, seeing his mocking smile tonight. John began to hiss and moan behind her signaling that the end was near. She hated she'd missed what was usually some pretty good sex. Tonight, all she could see was that smile. That mocking, sarcastic, *I killed your son and only got two years, so take that* kind of smile.

"Mmm, shit! Whew!" John exclaimed as he filled his condom. He slumped over on her back and fought for breath. The best orgasms damn near kill a man, and this was a good one.

"Okay," she said and rolled away. He fell beside her and began to blink and yawn. Snores soon followed but she was wide awake with her thoughts. She fought her sleep knowing one of those haunting nightmares was waiting on her like Freddie Kruger.

11:00 PM

"Where all the hoes?" Hot Rod, asked seeing mostly dudes in the line in front of the club.

"Hoes get in free before eleven. These the hoes we don't want since they got their own money," Mann explained. "Free hoes fuck quicker!"

"True," Fresh agreed and nodded. It was true to a degree since most women who worked and took care of themselves tended to be a little more selective. The ones asking for drinks, weed and waffles, were quicker to fuck.

Carlos felt a conflict from what he came from to what he come to believe. He grew up loving the profanity-laden music blaring through the sound system but gave it up as a Muslim. While some Muslims debated if music was permissible or not, he just chose to abstain. Not only could he do without the negative, misogynistic lyrics he just found better use of his time.

Now he enjoyed the melodic recitation of the Qur'an. That didn't stop his head from nodding to the funky beat. Didn't stop him from posting up at a table with another cold beer in his hand or from accepting the next blunt in rotation.

"I heard ole Herman was down there with you? He said he was knocking niggas off?" Mann questioned. A dude from the neighborhood just returned from doing a bid as well, and had war stories. According to him, he was a cross between a bear and gorilla while in prison.

"Is that what he said?" Carlos asked and laughed. It was pretty funny since Herman was in prison getting niggas off instead. He probably was gay before he went to prison but being around all those men brought it out.

"He said you was running with the Moozlimz, too!" Fresh asked, cocking his head as if it was a dare.

"Is that what he said?" he repeated. He wasn't necessarily embarrassed about his faith. He just knew they wouldn't understand. That's why he would just hang out with them tonight and go to the masjid tomorrow. Hang out and turn up tonight and be righteous in the morning.

"I heard it's crazy down that road!" Hot Rod said with an audible timbre of fear in his voice. He had absolutely no business in the streets doing street shit because he was terrified of going to jail. The exact trait that makes dudes tell on everyone and everything they know when they get pinched. His own mother was in trouble for her tax schemes if he ever got knocked because he was going to tell on her, too.

"Yeah," Carlos said and sighed, drifting back to that first day in prison. Seeing weak and white plucked away off the bat. Hearing the screams from beatings, stabbings, and rapes, echoing in the night. Seeing the empty eyes of a rape victim the next morning. One white boy from middle Georgia caught a couple of years for breaking in houses. All he wanted was some new video games but ended up being passed around like a blunt. He chose swinging from the end of a bed rather than another night of that. He already hated black men, but he really hated being raped by them.

"Is that Lil Los?" a scantily dressed hood rat asked as she led a flock of rats up to the table.

"Sup Ki-Ki," he replied and stood so she could hug him.

"That's right. My nigga fresh out the joint. One of y'all hoes need to go on and break him off!" Mann almost demanded like he was in charge of their vaginas. They were community coochie and belonged to all.

"Been wanting to fuck him!" a cute little nineteen-year old named Ally announced and stepped forward. Carlos remembered that illegal sexual intercourse was a big deal in Islam, but man, he been wanting to fuck her, too. Maybe he could fuck her tonight, then take her to the masjid with him. He was going to need a wife, so why not teach her Islam and clean her up like he was cleaned up?

"Uh oh!" Fresh cheered at the connection. He grabbed a rat for himself and hit the dance floor. Even if he didn't get laid, at least he could get his grind on.

"Come on!" Ally demanded and pulled Carlos off his chair and onto the dance floor. She turned around and began bouncing her ass against his instant erection. It was foreplay in the hood.

Carlos let out another sigh and accepted his fate. He agreed with himself to drink, smoke and have sex with her, then back to the deen in the morning. He'd missed all his prayers since getting out but would get back to it at dawn.

2:00 AM Saturday

Marlo lost the battle to stay awake and Freddy was right there waiting.

"*Boy, why my door unlocked!*" *Marlo fussed when she pulled her burglar bar open without a key. Chances are no one would hit their house out of fear and respect for Thad and his mother in that order. Not the regular neighborhood thieves any way because crack heads don't discriminate between friend or foe, family or friends. They don't just burn bridges, they steal them and smoke them in their pipes.*

Marlo sucked her teeth and shook her head at the rumble of bass coming from his room. She rushed into her room and bathroom to relieve herself of the hour stuck in rush hour traffic.

"*Whew!*" *she sighed, then let out a giggle at the loud sound of herself peeing. She saw a meme online stating that women with good pussy peed loud. She wiped, stood, and washed her hands. She frowned curiously at her reflection and reflected. She knew something was amiss because her begging ass son hadn't coming begging for something.*

He worked a little job and chipped in, but was like a child when it came to food. She decided what to eat for lunch each day with him in mind. She would only eat half of her food so she would stay fine and so he could eat the balance. He usually met her at the door but today he didn't come out of his room.

"*Better not have that nasty girl in there!*" *she fussed and stomped down the hallway. She stopped short of busting in just in case he did have Dana in there again.* "*Thaddeus Johnson, you open this door right now!*"

She banged on the door hurting her tiny hand but got no reply. She turned the knob and pushed the door open. The lingering smell of weed explained him laid out on the bed with his mouth open but didn't explain the blood. The coppery smell of blood permeated the air just beneath the weed.

"*Thad?*" *she pleaded in contradiction to the large pool of blood beneath his head. She was more angry than sad and demanded her dead son to* "*Get up, this instant! You ain't even lock the burglar bars!*"

Thaddeus was silent, as dead people tend to be. Even when she shook his foot and leg, then climbed on top of him in a futile attempt to wake the dead. A feat that hasn't been pulled off since Jesus by the will of his Lord.

"No, baby! Noooooo!" *she wailed and woke John beside her.*

"What's wrong, baby?" he said even though he already knew. She had nightmares on a regular basis, so regular he began spending the night a lot less often.

"Yeah, I'm sorry. He was laughing at me! Laughing at Thaddeus!" she pouted and whined with her lip poked out.

"No, he's not. This is crazy. You gotta let it go, Marlo. How long you gonna torture yourself? Huh?" he asked insensitively, while rubbing her sensitive vagina.

Marlo was too stunned by the question to reply. Out loud anyway, because internally she was spewing a profanity laced tirade. She would never let it go. No, not ever.

She let out a frustrated sigh as he mounted her and pushed inside. She watched the ceiling fan rock in unison with his short, choppy stroke. He didn't bother to kiss or caress, just hump and grunt. Marlo felt lower than any other point ever in her life. They weren't in a relationship, yet he was inside of her raw as if they were. He reminded her of that fact with a final grunt and pulled out to ejaculate on her stomach.

"Mm, shit!" he gasped and rolled off. Seconds later, he was snoring once again and once again she was alone in her pain.

"Let it go?" she huffed, shaking her head and breaking up with him in her head.

5:30 AM

"That nigga drunk!" Mann cheered happily as Carlos stumbled from the club with his arm wrapped around Ally. No one he knew got a college degree or promotion at work, so being pissy drunk was something to be celebrated.

Carlos was pretty drunk, but the orange predawn glow still registered. It was time to pray but he was in no condition to stand before his Lord. He let out a sigh at missing yet another prayer and the sins still to be committed once they reached the rundown motel.

The four couples pushed the older Caprice to its limit when they piled inside. The kisses and gropes continued as Mann bent a few corners to the motel. Four couples equaled two double rooms for the group low on cash, morals, and shame. Fresh and a girl whose name he didn't get, accompanied Carlos and Ally while Fresh, Mann and the other two girls got the other.

Men are the protectors and maintainers of women, Carlos thought to himself as he watched Ally and the girl with no name take off their clothes. The strip show was over in seconds since neither wore much clothing to begin with.

"What you doing my nigga?" Fresh demanded when he saw Carlos didn't budge. His lowers desires battled with his belief and newfound morals. He almost wanted to cry when his base self beat his higher self and helped him undress. Two years without a woman was more than he could stand. The devil whispered that Allah forgives again and again, causing him to nod in agreement. He still planned to get right today, just a little detour inside the girl.

"I ain't got no rubber," he said, thankful for a valid excuse not to enter the forbidden vagina.

"You don't need no rubber cuz I'm already pregnant. Going to Grady next week to get it out of me," she explained without explaining she'd just given birth a few months ago. She reached down and placed him near the entrance of her body.

"Wow!" Carlos heard himself say when he practically fell to the bottom of her well. Her vagina had an open floor plan without any walls whatsoever.

"It's good?" Ally asked even though she really couldn't feel much. They called him Lil Los because of his short stature. That extended into his underwear as well with a penis proportional to his height, aka short.

"Mmhm," he replied truthfully. It probably would have been a lot better with walls but two years is a long time. So long Carlos realized that he could do without it. Pussy cost him more than he could ever get back. His friend, big brother, and mentor all in one. "Damn it!"

"I know!" Ally giggled, taking it as a compliment. A few humps and pumps later, Carlos began to moan. He went rigid and released pent up sexual frustrations. With that out the way, he could go back to being righteous again. As soon as he woke up that is, because a good nut will put a man to sleep quicker than Thanksgiving dinner. Ally had nowhere to go no time soon and fell asleep as well.

Fresh and his date screwed ten minutes longer and joined the snoring contest already in progress. Checkout time wasn't until 11:00 AM, giving them all a much needed rest.

6:00 AM

"Un uh," Marlo declined when John tried to roll over on top and inside of her. He often got a quick nut before jumping in the shower to head to work.

"You sure?" he proposed, while tapping his thick erection, on her thigh.

"I think my period coming," she lied to turn him off.

"I'll take a little head then," he offered as a consolation. The only thing she sucked was her teeth before she rolled off the bed. She went into her bathroom and sat on the toilet to pee. He stomped by and hopped in the shower complaining and grumbling. She made sure to flush so the rush of hot water would give him something to complain about.

He came out the bathroom completely naked as if to show her what she was missing out on. She agreed as she stole a glance at his dangling meat but was done with him. His words that she *"get over it"* put a snarl on her face while she watched him.

"Too late now! I tried to give you some!" he laughed, seeing her fixated on his dick. He pulled his boxers up as if punishing her. "I may swing through at lunch and give you a little. Maybe."

"Don't do me no favors. Matter fact, come through at lunch so you can get your shit. This—" she said, pointing her finger back and forth between the two of them "—is over with."

"You tripping," he said, twisting his lips in disbelief. He finished dressing and headed to the door. He knew he would have to swing back during lunch with food and dick to fix whatever was wrong with her.

7:30 AM

Deputy Jenkins was too arrogant to be alarmed when all talking came to an abrupt halt as soon as he walked into the briefing room. He tilted his head a little higher in pride since his coworkers were obviously in awe of him. He'd had meaningless sex with the three female deputies, even though only one of them actually looked like a female. Still, the other two had vaginas, so he'd went in.

He could feel the stares and whispers, while sipping his coffee. The captain walked in to start the briefing as he sipped his coffee. He didn't think much of the man and planned not to even listen to him. Instead, he watched replays of his record setting day the day before on his phone.

"Excuse me, Deputy Jenkins? I hate to interrupt whatever it is that you're doing," the captain said with a hint of sarcasm.

"I'm listening, Cap," he said without looking up. Had he looked up he would have seen two other deputies flanking him ready to pounce.

"Well, hear this," he said with a smile. It was an honor to arrest the pretty, playboy who bedded his department crush. "You're under arrest! Get him out of here!"

"What! Quit playing! Get off me!" he demanded, while his coworkers clapped and cheered. He bitched and moaned while they dragged him away. So much for breaking his own record today.

11:05 AM

"A'ight, my nigga!" Fresh shouted at the incessant knocking on the door. The maid was eager to change the nasty beds so she could go home. "Say, Los. Get up, shawty. Time to push."

Carlos frowned up at his friend trying to place the place he woke up in. He glanced at the sleeping girl next to him with a line of drool forming a pool on her pillow. Fresh held his finger to his mouth to shush his friend so he wouldn't wake the girls.

He knew it wasn't right but still eased out of the bed and quietly put his clothes back on. The two eased out of the room as Mann and Hot Rod did the same. It was their standard M.O to leave thots sleeping in motel rooms. The four friends climbed back in the car to make their escape.

"He hit?" Mann asked Fresh as he pulled from the parking lot.

"Fo' about two minutes!" he cracked up and said, rolling the next blunt up.

"After two years, I'm surprised he lasted that long!" Hot Rod tossed in.

"'Shit, it's been longer than two years since he wasn't getting much ass 'fo he got locked up!" Mann cracked.

"Yeah, I was! I was smashing Dana!" Carlos shot back in his own defense and regretted it instantly. The car went quiet except for the engine knocking and bad CV joints clicking when he turned.

Everyone present knew that whatever had happened between him and Thad had something to do with Dana. Everyone present had also smashed Dana at least once since Carlos went away. One of them could possibly be her youngest child's daddy, but so could a number of other men.

The blunt passed around the silence as they rode back to their hood. Mann made a quick detour to the local liquor store. Carlos shook his head at the thought of more alcohol but the blunt he smoked assured him it would be okay. *I'll just hang out with his friends over the weekend, then Monday, I'ma get back on my deen,* he told himself. It sounded reasonable, so he nodded in agreement as Mann came out with several cases of beer. He got back behind the wheel and pulled out into traffic.

11:41 AM

Marlo almost grabbed her pistol in conjunction with the knocking on her burglar door since she wasn't expecting company. It was in her purse on top of her keys. The local burglars always knock before kicking the door in. She heard the small voice in his singsong tone and went to open it for her grandson.

"Hey, Miss Marlo. Donquatashawn wanted to see you. Been talkin' 'bout his granny all morning!" she lied as Marlo scooped the giggling boy into a firm grandma hug.

"Is that right, Don-q, um, baby?" she asked, failing to get the name right for once. She knew the little rat was lying since she was dressed slightly more slutty than normal. The tiny halter-top showed slight stretch marks and nipples. An equally small pair of shorts displayed her wrinkled stomach and camel toe. "Did you bring a bag?"

"Of what?" the piss poor mother asked for the second time today. Her own mother had asked about a bag for her newborn when she left her home with her.

"Nothing," Marlo said since it would be easier to run out and grab whatever the toddler needed than trying to explain. Not to mention it gave her a chance to get out and show off her grandson. That sure beat moping around the house mourning her child all over again. Seeing Carlos again ripped the scabs off her heart just as they finally began to form. It's impossible to heal if the scab keeps coming off.

"Guess, you not coming to the cookout, huh?" Dana asked, scrunching her face up and shaking her head. "Probably not."

Marlo was about to ask what cookout since she loved a good cookout. She wouldn't eat just anyone's potato salad but loved her some ribs. She tilted her head upward and got the answer for herself from the activity across the street.

"Carlos home," she explained with a faux sad face. Little's, however his name was pronounced, presence prevented Marlo from jumping on the girl. The thought of not being able to see her son's twin would literally kill her. She had no one else to love or love her back.

"I see," she said as Mann pulled the bucket to a squealing stop in front of the house. She missed whatever it was the girl said before she twisted her nasty little ass across the street. A cold chill of hate ran up her spine when she watched her grandson's mother embrace her son's killer.

"Why you ain't tell me when you was coming home?" Dana purred and gave him a squeeze. His face morphed into a question mark as he pondered the question. Taking responsibility for the *"incident"* was one thing but it was still her fault. He had no intention on ever dealing with the girl again. She did look good though.

"Um," was the best he could come up with. She did feel good though, so he squeezed her back. No telling how long they would have stood there hugging but he broke it off when he saw Miss Marlo giving him the evil eye from across the street. "Come on. Let's go 'round back."

If looks could kill, the two would have dropped dead on the spot as she shot daggers into their backs. They received the opposite reaction when they reached the backyard.

"There go my baby!" Nita cheered and jumped up from her lawn chair. Her forty-year old body jiggled in the age inappropriate clothing she'd selected. Even her son zoomed in on the bouncing breasts, then quickly turned away since they were his mother's bouncing breast.

"Hey, mama," he replied, feeling embarrassed by her appearance. Her outfit was almost the same as Dana's just in a different color. Her shorts were pulled up tightly to show off her vagina and her nipples pressed through her halter-top, as well. He vowed to call his mother to Islam when he came home, but here she was passing him a blunt.

"Smoke something!" she cheered and danced. This wasn't the time or place to preach, so he accepted it and took a pull. "See you got lil mama with you. She been checking on you the whole time you been gone!"

"Mmhm," Dana nodded proudly. All she did was ask *"how Los"* whenever she saw her coming or going. Most of the time, she was with yet another dude.

"You wanna fix him a burger? The ribs ain't going on 'til later," Nita asked so she could finally have a moment with her son. Dana almost turned her nose up at the notion of serving a man but caught on and agreed. She wasn't going to fix his food but would give them some space.

"Sup, mama?" Carlos asked since he caught it too. Especially since Dana just walked over to the next blunt in rotation and slid in.

"You," she smiled and looked her son over. He had definitely matured in the two years he'd been gone. What she couldn't see was the internal changes he'd made. His heart was no longer black, but every missed prayer, toke of smoke, sip of beer and touch of a woman added a stain on his heart. It would grow black with every sin until completely black and dead.

"Have you seen Miss Marlo?" Nita asked and sighed. "You know we ain't talked since, you know."

"Naw, I ain't seen her yet," he almost lied. He had seen her but didn't look at her. He knew he had to face her one day as part of his repentance he needed to apologize.

"You need to talk to her. You done told me you sorry 'bout what happened but did you tell her? That's who you need to say sorry to. She lost her child. I know I ain't the best mama in the world, but I would lay down and die if something happened to you. I can't even look her in her face no more!"

"Don't cry, mama," he pleaded, seeing a lone tear stream down her face. "I'ma go over there and talk to her. Tomorrow, okay?"

"Okay, baby. Make sure you do," she agreed and knocked the tear away. "You ready to eat?"

"I need to hop in the shower first," he said since he could still smell Ally on him. His mother admired his growth as he walked into the house.

1:00 PM

"You just like your daddy!" Marlo giggled at her grandson. It was uncanny how much the child was like his father. He had all of his mannerisms even though they would never meet. Even Thaddeus's father popped in and out but he would never get to see him.

"Dada," the child repeated as if he knew he was supposed to have one.

"Dada," she repeated, using everything she had not to cry. It was deja vu when her grandson pointed at the toy store as they walked through the mall. "Want a toy?"

The child nodded and pointed as she led him inside to pick out whatever he wanted. She was unable to prevent the tears from falling when he picked out a truck just like his father used to do. She got herself together by the time she met Janice in the food court.

"Hey, girl. Is this your grand baby?" Janice cooed and scooped the toddler off his feet. He looked to his grandmother curiously since he wasn't accustomed to affection.

"Yes, that's little, um, Thaddeus," she decided. His real name was too much for her, so she would call him Thad from now on.

"Well, hello there, Mr. Thad," she sang and sat him down. "S and S?"

"Sure! I could go for a pizza-stuffed burger with a heap of parmesan fries!" she said, taking a break from her diet.

"Uh oh! Not you eating a stuffed burger! You sure you don't want no black bean burger? Or veggie?" Janice dared. She was a proud big girl with no need to diet since men love big fine just as much as they love slim fine.

"Nah, I'm trying to get fine like you so I can find myself a new man," she said, breaking the news of the breakup.

"A new one! What's wrong with the one you got?" she reeled in disbelief.

"Wrong? What's right with him! Just sick of him! Ugh!" she grunted and shivered.

"Good, cuz he kept trying holla at me! Every time I been around, y'all he wink anytime you blink," Janice admitted.

"I seen him. Saw you frown up at him, too. Most times women would giggle or wink back. I'm glad you kept it real," Marlo replied.

"One, cuz I'm your friend for real. And two, that's just nasty! That thang between his legs gonna get him in trouble one day," she said unknowing today was that day.

"Chile, that's the only thing I'm going to miss about him," she laughed honestly. He was plenty handsome but wore a smug look that made him ugly. She shivered once more at the thought of him.

1:30 PM

"I can't eat this. This is what we feed the inmates!" Jenkins fussed when a tray was slid into his cell. All deputies have to start out at the jail so he knew he would be held in protective custody away from the other inmates. He also knew how bad the jail food was since it was jail food. He always wondered how people survived on it for weeks, months, and years. He was about to find out since he was charged with sodomy and other serious sex related crimes.

"And you are an inmate!" a female deputy shot back with malice on her breath. She shoved the tray inside the slot so viciously the beans sloshed into the applesauce.

"Hey!" he griped since he was going to eat the sauce but not the beans. "What is your problem?"

"You!" she shot back and stormed off. Her angry strides made her large ass shift, catching the womanizer's eye. He was about to think how she looked like she had some good-good, wet-wet until he remembered she did.

"Oh yeah!" he chuckled as he recalled hitting her from the back then sneaking out when she went to sleep. She didn't take kindly to being hit and quit. It was ten years ago, but it still stung. He may be laughing but actually, the joke was on him since she was going home at the end her shift. He was already at home where he would be for a long time to come.

Coercing the daughter of two prominent lawyers to blow him to avoid arrest was going to cost him. Her gags and crying during the blow jog could be clearly heard on the surveillance footage. So was her breaking down in heaving sobs after he left.

1:45 PM

Carlos literally had to force himself out of the shower. It was the most peace and privacy he had to shower in years, even with a full-fledged party going on in the backyard. Not to mention being able to adjust the water just how he wanted it. In prison, you got what they gave you. Either too hot or too cold.

"Shit! I mean shoot!" he corrected since the new Carlos AKA Hasan didn't curse much. He still hated having to deal with his old friends and old life even if it was just for one more day. "Going to the masjid tomorrow!"

Carlos dressed in his new clothes while regretting his decision to come home. He should have paroled out to his grandmother's house where he didn't know any one. Where no one knew him and he could be whoever he wanted to be. Namely, Hasan Muwakil, the Muslim. Because everyone was waiting on Lil Los to come back outside to drink, smoke and turn up. He wanted to turn them down but felt like he owed them. He would repay that debt today, then get back on the straight path tomorrow. He nodded in agreement to his plan but still forgot to say In sha Allah.

"Here he go! Come dance with yo' mama!" Nita cheered when her son emerged from the house. The size of the party had doubled in size so she wanted a little attention before his friends swooped him away.

"Okay," he said with a defeated sigh. Seeing his mother dressed and dancing like a teen scraped against his soul. She was twerking and popping and dropping just like the younger thots. After all, the only difference between a young thot and an old thot is twenty years and perhaps some vaginal elasticity.

"Uh oh. Uh oh!" Nita cheered and shook. Shook and twerked along with her son to the latest jam coming through the speakers. It didn't take long until the rhythm hit him and he did the dances from two years ago. Jail is like a time machine, so to him, it was still 2015 when he went away.

4:45 PM

"Hmph," Marlo huffed when she pulled onto her street and saw not only had the party not ended it had actually grown. She contained her protest to her own mind since she had her grandson with her. She knew she could keep him as long as there was a party going on. There was always a party going on somewhere, which made her think about keeping him fulltime.

Dana certainly wouldn't mind since that would free her up to sling her public privates all over the city. She would too, but tonight they belonged to Carlos. His friends wouldn't mind since they had it for the two years he'd been gone.

Her grandson had fallen asleep from the movement of the car so she unstrapped him from his car seat and carried him to the door. It was a little tricky trying to open the burglar bar and front doors holding the child. Luckily, she had plenty of practice from decades of shopping sprees. Once inside she laid the toddler down on the sofa and went back for his new clothes and toys from the car. Both would be staying there since the ratchet girl's house was the Bermuda Triangle for new shit. Everything she ever sent over there came up missing.

"Whaaat?" Marlo said and laughed upon hearing her seldom used home phone ring. She so rarely used it, she had to check her contacts to give someone the number. For that reason, she let it ring and continued what she was doing. Her curiosity was sparked by the third time it rung prompting her to pick up. "Hello?"

"You have a collect call from an inmate at the Fulton County Jail, 'John Jenkins'. To accept, press one. To decline, press two. To block..."

"Hello?" Marlo asked with the same curiosity that made her answer.

"Thank God! I've been calling you all day! Where the hell you been?" John demanded like he was in a position to make demands. He hadn't got the memo yet but they were broken up.

"Um," Marlo said in confusion. She had been confused as to why he would be calling collect from jail, but his demands really threw her for a loop. "Not that I answer to you, but I took my grandson to the mall. I hope that's to your liking."

"I guess. Look, I got arrested for some bull shit. I won't be able to see a judge until Monday. Make sure you're there with your deed to make my bond," he ordered. That too was pretty confusion to Marlo.

"Um," she repeated since she couldn't find the words she was looking for. A moment later, they came to her brain and rushed out of her mouth. "Just why would I do that? I'm not dealing with you ever again. Whenever you work out whatever you got going on, your stuff is packed right by the front door."

"Listen, bitch. I have some serious shit going on. Don't fucking play with me! Trust me, you don't want to get on my bad side!"

"Fuck both sides, bottom, top, um, middle! I got something for your ass you come around here!" Marlo said, looking towards the sofa table near the front door. On it was her purse. In it was her pistol.

"Bit—shit!" he fussed when she hung up. He called right back and got no answer. Marlo did listen to the complete instructions this time, so he was blocked the next time he called. "Bitch!"

10:30 PM

"Me and Jose finna go to the movies," Nita announced as the party began to wind down. After a day of eating, smoking and drinking it was time for most people to hit the club.

"We are?" Jose asked with a confused frown. He'd invited her home for sex and didn't know anything about any movies. He wasn't quite swift enough to catch the woman might not want to tell her son that. She looked at him and shook her head. If he hadn't had such good weed, she might have changed her mind.

"Plus, I know you and lil bit want to be alone," she said with a wink that made Dana giggle and snuggle up against him.

"Oh," Carlos replied since he really didn't want to be alone with the girl. Once again, he let out a sigh and gave in to what everyone else wanted. "Okay."

Nita left with her other boyfriend leaving the two in the midst of an awkward silence. Not breaks the ice like a good shot of pussy so Dana offered him one.

"Let's go to your room," she said and got up to lead the way. He recalled the good times and good sex they'd had in that room as he got up. He looked down at her ass and noticed it was wider and fatter than when he left. Two years of back shots and a second child will do that.

It was just like old times when Dana immediately began to strip as soon as they got to the room. It was just like new times when Carlos followed and stripped out of his clothes as well. Dana climbed on the bed and spread her legs. Carlos caught a slight whiff of the sex she'd had earlier but he had an erection and overlooked it.

"You miss this good pussy, huh?" she asked hopefully as he climbed between her legs and rolled a condom on.

"Um, yeah," he replied, preparing to enter. It didn't take much prep since she was slippery wet and loose. He noticed it was nothing like he remembered, but she was a good actor and moaned and groaned, thrashed like he was killing it.

Two years is a long time and vagina is vagina, so it didn't take long for him to get fully involved. He lifted her legs folded her into *"the buck"*. The room filled with the sounds and smell of rough sex. Yeah, two years is a long time and he did great to last more than two minutes.

"Argh! Shit! Whew! Mmm," he said, while going through convulsions and spasms of orgasm.

"It was good?" she pleaded. Dana hadn't finished high school but was smart enough to understand her only strength lay between her legs. The plump mound of flesh was all she had to offer a man.

"Yeah," he responded because it had been two years. A lot had changed in that time besides the size of her vagina. He wanted to drift into his thoughts but her incessant chatter wouldn't allow it. He nodded and "mmhm-ed" along to whatever she was talking about until something registered. He sat straight up and asked, "What you just say?"

"Huh?" she asked since she wasn't quite sure herself. Even she knew she had the tendency to rattle absentmindedly just to fill the space. "Oh, about Thaddeus? Just wish he could see his son grow up. I wish y'all ain't fall out."

"I wish we didn't either. I wish he never started dissing me. We were 'sposed to be boys," Carlos said meaning every syllable. The pain was evident in his voice but it was about to get worse. Turn up, like they say.

"Thad? Talking shit about you? Boy, stop! He loved you! Said you was his lil' brother!" She sat up and declared. "Who told you he was talking shit about you? They a damn lie!"

Carlos strained his face and memory and clearly recalled the conversation that led to the incident. Right here in this same bed, naked after sex. He let it replay in his head and it made even less sense now than it did then. He found it hard to believe but had been persuaded by the power of the pussy. Victorious vaginas had vanquished better men than he since the beginning of time.

"Get out," he said so softly it didn't sound like the command that it was. So softly, she wasn't sure if she heard what she thought she heard.

"Huh?" she asked since *"excuse me"* wasn't a part of her limited vocabulary. She just knew he didn't tell her to get out after he got off, like so many other men had.

"Get dressed and get out," he repeated just as calmly. The realization that he'd killed his friend for nothing squeezed his chest and made breathing difficult.

"You just want yo' dick sucked!" she said, twisting her lips. She dipped her head to give him some head but he pushed her away.

"No, I just want you to go and never come back. Don't ever come near me or my mama again!" he insisted.

"Fuck you and yo' mama!" she shot back and leaped from the bed. She cursed them both as she scrambled to get dressed. She couldn't locate her panties from flinging them somewhere and dressed without them. Luckily, they came five to a pack because she ran through them on a regular.

Carlos had secretly shed many a tear since the incident but never like the chest heaving, snot out the nose, bawling he did now. His heart wrenching wails could be heard all throughout the empty house.

The crying stopped just as suddenly as it began when he realized what needed to be done. He wiped his face with his hands and put his clothes back on. He slid his new tennis shoes over his bare feet and left his room. He stepped out on the front porch and looked across the street. The darkness of Marlo's house was the only thing that prevented him from walking over there and giving her the apology she deserved.

The one she desperately needed to heal. She would have thanked him for it and for saving her from another nightmare of finding her dead son.

"Tomorrow," he said and sighed, then went back inside the house. Again, he forgot to say In sha Allah since tomorrow isn't promised to anyone. And despite your best efforts, you cannot will unless God wills.

1:30 AM Sunday

"Shit!" Carlos muttered when another deep yawn shook his body. He knew what fate awaited him when he went to sleep. He knew it was the devil and not Freddie waiting to give him another bad dream.

He smoked more weed hoping to either stay awake or fall so deeply asleep, he could hide from the devil. Not happening because the only refuge from the devil is with God. People who turn to people or intoxicants only compound their problems. There is no reward for good except good, so what about sin. All good is from God. Whatever bad happens is from our own hands.

He let out a defeated sigh as drifted off to sleep.

"Called me lame!" Carlos fumed, as he exhaled a plume of weed smoke. Meanwhile, Shaiton whispered sinister suggestions into his ear like sweet nothings. The devil's job is to make wicked deeds seem fair. That's why he grabbed his gun to go check his friend, mentor and surrogate big brother.

Carols stepped off his porch and marched across the street. They were close enough to have an open door policy, but today he knocked since this was a formal visit.

"Who?" Thaddeus called from inside his room. Working nights allowed him to sleep during the day but having the house to himself, allowed him to have girls over and gone before his mama came home. He laughed to himself, thinking about his mother sniffing the air for scents of sex when she came in. She was the proud owner of a clean, well-maintained vagina and could smell the opposite from a mile away.

"*Shit!*" *he fussed when the knocking continued and he realized he would have to get out of bed. Hopefully whoever it was, had a vagina to make up for being inconvenienced. "Los? Why you knocking on the door?"*

Thaddeus pushed the burglar door latch and it came right open since he never locked it when he was home. His mother was a lot more cautious and kept it locked when she was home. She kept her keys right on top of her pistol in her purse near the front door. He teased her about that all the time, knowing she wouldn't bust a grape let alone a burglar.

"*Cuz, I need to...*" *his said, but big speech was put on pause when Thad began walking back to his room to lay back down. He felt even more disrespected as followed him to make his point. "Yeah, like I was saying. I heard you was talking shit about me!"*

"*Probably was,*" *Thaddeus chuckled, as he plopped down on his bed. "Let me guess. Dana told you this, huh?"*

"*Yeah!*" *he shot back. In his mind, it was proof that she was telling the truth. Truth was Thaddeus knew she was a troublemaker and expected it when he saw his partner hook up with her. "Said you said I was lame!"*

"*Shit, you is if you believe anything that bitch say. You know she running around saying she pregnant from me,*" *he sighed.*

"*Nigga, you lame!*" *he shot back and pulled the pistol to prove it. Thaddeus began to laugh hysterically at his friend holding the gun in his shaking hand. The laughter stung so much, he pulled the hammer back cocking the gun. "You think it's a game?"*

"*Yes,*" *Thaddeus laughed as his friend struggled to hold the large gun in his small hand. He adjusted his grip putting a hair too much pressure on its hair trigger. The gun sounded like a cannon blast when it went off in the small room.*

"*Oh shit! My bad!*" *he frantically apologized. He just knew big brother was about to beat him up for shooting the gun in his room. Probably would have if not for the strange look in his eye. That far away, unfocused gaze of the dead. "Thad? Thad! Oh shit!"*

Carlos grabbed the phone to call 9-1-1 but realized his friend was gone. He quickly hung up because it was he who'd sent him wherever it was he went. His DNA and prints were on the phone when he sat it down. He ran around the house in a panic trying to figure out his next move. The best he could come up with was to go home and pretend like nothing happened. He would just play dumb when asked if he saw or heard anything. There were no witnesses, so no one could say what happened one way or the other.

"Where Thad at?" Mann asked as he and Fresh smoked with Carlos on the porch a few hours later. They couldn't go inside since Nita always wanted to hit the weed. Not to mention, she never wore enough clothes and it bothered him seeing his friends looking at her tits and ass.

"I'on know," Carlos said, sounding so phony, even he frowned along with his friends. None of them thought much so none of them thought anything about it. The weed rotated in conjunction with inane conversation about rappers, actors and chicks with fat asses.

"That's who I wanna fuck," Mann admitted when they watched Marlo turn on the street. Carlos began to hold his breath at that point. "Don't tell Thad I said that!"

"She is fine, though!" Fresh cosigned when Marlo stepped out of her car, wearing a snug business suit skirt and blouse. Her panty lines where visible from across the street and all eyes tuned in.

"Hey, Carlos, fellas!" she smiled and waved at the boys before turning to go inside. The round ass shifted side to side as she climbed the stairs. She let out a little chuckle knowing the boys were looking at her backside.

Carlos tried to hold his breath but realized he already had been holding it. He let it out and traded it for another. He braced himself for the outburst, but it didn't come. Not yet anyway since Marlo rushed straight to the bathroom to relieve herself. She had been telling herself for the last fifteen minutes of her commute that fly girls don't pee on themselves. She barely made it and got to keep her fly girl status.

"Hmph," Carlos grunted to himself. He just realized that the whole thing didn't even happen. It was just a bad dream he had from smoking too much weed. He shook his head and began to laugh at himself. "I'm tripping."

"About what?" Mann asked but before he could answer Marlo busted out her door hysterically.

"Help! Someone shot my baby!" she pleaded. The sound of her screams shook his very soul and sent a shiver up his spine. He could hear that scream to this day as vividly as he did that day. To make matters worse, she ran straight across the street to him. "Help me, Carlos! We gotta wake him up!"

"I don't, um, ain't see..." he explained as she hugged him tightly. The scream echoed again and woke him again as it had many nights since it happened.

7:00 AM

"Shit!" Carlos fussed when the bad dream snatched him from a fitful sleep. He let out a sigh seeing he had missed his dawn prayer once again. He thought about making ablution to pray but felt the effects of all the weed he had smoked. The ritual purification doesn't clean away intoxicants since they are forbidden in the first place. Not to mention he was in a state of sexual impurity from the nasty girl. Muslims must bathe between sex and prayer, but that's for married people. He wondered if there was an injunction for sex with thots.

"Shit!" he repeated since this was the day he was supposed to get it together. To get back on his deen, but it was starting out on the wrong foot once again. Being a Muslim is not just what you do, it's who you are. Every second, every breath, worshipping your Lord who created you.

"Carlos! You home?" Nita called out as she came through the door. Jose proved once again that he was no gentleman and pulled off before she even reached the front door. He made his point last night and again this morning with rough sex.

"In here!" he called out and went to her in the living room. Nita looked just like she had been sexed all night. She had bags under her eyes and her hair was all over her head. She winced with pain from her battered vagina when she plopped down on the sofa. "Sup, mama."

"You!" she said, smiling at her handsome son. She made a big production as she produced the neatly rolled blunt she had swiped from Jose's ashtray. She reasoned it wasn't technically stealing since she had his semen swimming around in her. "Fire it up!"

"Un uh, I ain't smoking no more!" he firmly declined and went on to explain. "I'm Muslim now. I took my Shahadah in prison. I ain't 'sposed smoke or drink or have sex—"

"Muslims can't have sex!?" she reeled. "It's bad enough you can't eat no pork skins, but you can't fuck either? See, that's why I couldn't be no moozlim!"

"Muslim, and yeah we can fu—have sex. Just gotta be married. I been smoking and drinking just to be thankful for errbody coming to see me and holding me down, but I gotta get right. Get to the masjid..." he explained, leaving out the part about crossing the street to apologize and beg for forgiveness.

"So, you smoke with yo' friends, but not with yo' mama? I'm the one carried you in my belly. It was me who pushed yo' big head out they pussy! I'm the one—"

"Okay, mama! Last one! No more after this! After this, I'm getting back on my deen!" he insisted. None of that meant much to Nita who was just happy to get her way. She gloated internally as her son lit the weed and took a pull.

"So, since you a moozlim now, you gonna be blowing yo'self up and running people down in trucks?" she asked sincerely since that's all she saw about Muslims. For whatever reason, media exclusively showed the atrocities committed by so-called Muslims but never the good.

"Mama, that stuff ain't got nothing to with Islam! Matter fact, all that stuff is forbidden in Islam!" he defended. "Allah and our prophet

Muhammad, peace be upon him, never told us to do that. They both commanded us to do good on the earth. He, The Most High, set it in order. It's not for us to spoil that."

"So, why women gotta walk behind men?" she wanted to know. Carlos did too since that too had nothing to do with Islam.

"Beats me," he replied and shrugged. "See, sometimes people from other places mix Islam with whatever they culture is. They making they own religion when they do that, cuz that ain't Islam. Our prophet Muhammad, peace be upon him, said he was *only sent to perfect good manners*. So, anytime you see anything else just know that ain't Islam!"

"So, why women gotta wear all them clothes? They be looking all hot!"

"Not as hot as hell fire, but still, it's to protect women. Men are supposed to be the protectors and maintainers of women. Not to be exploited and used. Women dress like that cuz that's what men want. If men stepped up and be men, telling women not to dress like prostitutes, they wouldn't do it!"

"Well, I don't dress like no prostitute!" she shot back.

"Yes, you do, mama. But that's my fault cuz I allowed it," he explained.

"You ain't allow me to do nothing! I'm grown!" she shot back. "Shoot, I'm the one that pay all the bills around here! When you start paying them, then you can tell me what to wear!"

"That's a bet cuz that's exactly what I'm finna do. You trust me, right? You know I wouldn't tell you nothing bad, right?" he challenged.

"Yeah, I trust you," she said softly. Everything he said made sense, so why wouldn't she. The blunt found its way into a mayonnaise top turned ashtray and smoldered out as they talked. They talked for hours as he tried to answer all of her questions, while explaining Islam's number one tenant.

"There's nothing worthy of worship except for God who created us. That's the first commandment, ain't it?" he challenged.

"Yes," she agreed since she still knew the Ten Commandments by heart from church as a child. She had broken many of them and it never bothered her until that moment. A tear fell from her eye when she realized just how far she strayed from those commandments. "Can I go with you down to that temple?"

"Muslims don't have no temples, mama!" he laughed. "That's the nation of Islam and they ain't got nothing to do with Islam. All that white man is the devil bullshit!"

"Yeah, cuz ain't none of these devils running around here white," she huffed indignantly at the crazy notion.

"Islam ain't black, white or Arab. It's about worshipping God and doing good deeds. Period. And yes, you can come but..." he said and stopped, frowning at her mini dress and half shirt.

"Prolly should change, huh?" she giggled and stood. She held her head high and marched down the hall to her room.

Carlos had a night of sex too and went to take a shower of his own. An hour later, they were clean, sober and ready to take a positive step in their lives. There's no reward for good except good and they were ready to do good.

12:57 PM

The mother and son stepped from the house to drive over to the masjid on 14th Street. He stopped in his tracks and looked across the street.

"I need to holla at Miss Marlo," he said, nodding in agreement with himself.

"Yeah, you do," his mother said, agreeing too. She pressed her lips together in a proud smile and hugged him tightly. They looked at each other and nodded once more in confirmation. She watched her grown son march across the street to do the right thing.

12:59 PM

"Better not be John!" Marlo growled in response to her ringing doorbell. She sat her grandson's lunch in front of him and went to the door. Her heart dropped when she saw Carlos standing at the door. She turned to her purse as he turned to get a reassuring nod from his mama.

1:00 PM

It was exactly 48 hours after being released that Marlo opened her front door. She raised the pistol and shot him right between his eyes.

"Now, I'm over it."

THE END

The Ladies of D-Block
A Short Story by
Sa'id Salaam

When women are convicted of a crime in the great state of Georgia, they are sent to River Walk Correctional Facility to repay their debt to society. Some pay with a year or three, others owe a decade. Those with the most serious crimes are sent to D-block. A dangerous cell block designated for the most dangerous women.

These are their stories...

CHAPTER 1

LISA

"You don't have to go out, you know? You can have whatever you want right here. I'll do whatever you want," Lisa pleaded as her husband groomed himself for his date.

She heard the whining in her tone but didn't care. She wasn't too proud to beg, so she begged her husband to stay here with her. She had long ago lost all self esteem, so begging came easy. One of the downsides to letting people walk all over you, is that they'll walk all over you.

"Chill, Lisa. You act like I ain't coming back," Jalil huffed. Until recently, he was content with his older, chubby, yet cute wife. That was until her daughter returned from college.

Lisa was a single mother but raised her only child properly. Young Areeshia excelled in academics, dance, theatre and anything else she applied herself to. Steering clear of boys allowed her to concentrate on a future so bright, it made others squint. Dudes squinted too because the high yellow girl was pretty and pretty thick in all the right places.

Lisa was once fine like that, but let herself go in pursuit of her career. Areeshia's dad left when the girl reached five years of age and she reached three hundred of pounds. The woman looked at his departure as shedding two hundred pounds of dead weight. She worked doubles and triples and paid off her house in twelve years.

Lisa also doted on her daughter and was able to provide a full ride to college. She bought the girl a brand new car for the daily commute to school, but Areeshia begged to live on campus. The mother had reservations about sending her virginal, sheltered, and reserved child off on her own. In the end, she decided to let her daughter have the full college experience and moved her into the dorms.

The change came almost immediately. By that first Thanksgiving, there was an obvious change in the girl. She dressed a little sexier and spoke a lot more ghetto. Her once articulate speech was now laced with profanities and clipped words.

Areeshia went off to spring break and lost her virginity along with her mind. She tried drugs and liked it. Got some dick and liked it. Even ate a little pussy and what's not to like about eating pussy?

It may have been Areeshia Montgomery who went off to her freshman year of college, but it was Sexy Redd who came home for summer break. She made sure everyone knew her new name and tattooed it on her neck. A bright red tat to match the bright red hair she now favored.

School obviously slowed the girl down, but summer allowed her to party all the time. She stayed out days at a time, sexing different guys and gals at a time. Most people developed a durg of choice by that age, but she was a late bloomer, so she dabbled in all of them.

Of course her mother tried to intervene and reel her in, but the girl would snap so viciously, Lisa wondered if the girl would put her hands on her. She lost even more self esteem by letting the girl run all over her. She took from her purse so much, Lisa learned not to even carry cash anymore.

Both were relieved when summer ended and the girl went back to school. Only now, she was too turned up and turned out for school. She liked dick, dope, and dollars, so the strip club was the best place for her. Soon class took a backseat to shaking that ass.

The funny thing about going to college is they actually expect you to go to class. There weren't enough hours in a day for her to do both. Areeshia would have been responsible and buckled down in school. Her mom was a nurse and she intended to one up her and become a doctor. Only problem was Areeshia was now gone and Sexy Redd was calling the shots now. Sexy Redd said "fuck that school" and soon the school said the same thing about her, kicking her out of the dorms.

She spent the next six months living dick to mouth and couch to couch. Her third abortion took a toll on her and sent her home to recoup. Mama to the rescue like always, decided to take her in.

Of course, mama had rules in her house since she now had a husband at home. No boys, no smoking, no twerking, no nothing. And she was expected to get a job once she healed up.

It was bad enough Jalil didn't work, but it didn't matter since she didn't mind taking care of the man who took care of her lonely vagina. Chicks buy dick all the time, so she bought the whole man. A pet husband to walk in the park and take to church with her.

Well, Jalil and Areeshia didn't seem to notice each other at first. Each had a slight, envious aversion to the other. Neither wanted to share the benefits Lisa provided with the other. More for one meant less for the other the way these selfish motherfuckers saw it.

Lisa would leave them alone in the house while she went out to work. Someone had to pay the bills and keep the fridge filled. Plus Jalil liked kush, so he had to have an allowance for weed and munchies.

Areeshia smelled weed seeping through the door one day but didn't want to investigate. She may have had a little shame left, so she sent Sexy Redd down the hall to her mother's room.

She traded a twerk show for a few pulls on the weed, but it went no further. Only because her box was still healing from the near death, bootleg abortion. Jalil gave Lisa the best sex of her life when she got in that night. His dick was still hard from the daughter, so he took it out on the mother.

Well, it wasn't long until that hot pocket between her legs got right. The two freeloaders had become best friends as they chilled in the large, air conditioned home and ate all the free food in the fridge. Not to mention all the channels on the huge TV Lisa purchase

Soon they fucked. Sexy Redd's box was loose from all the miles she racked up in college but her body was banging compared to her mother. Her mother had some good, clean, tight pussy under that fupa, but he preferred the juicy loose between her daughter's tatted up thighs.

Lisa was a smart woman, even if a pushover. She noticed the couple of interlopers appeared to be an actual couple. It took all the courage she could muster and some she had to borrow before telling them both of her suspicions.

"Good! Cuz I'm tired of sneaking around. Yeah we get high and fuck! So what?" Sexy Redd demanded and stood like she was ready to fight.

Fight her own mother in her own home, over her own husband. "Your fat ass don't want no smoke!"

Lisa sulked away and lived life in a daze. Soon days turned to weeks and weeks into months.

Now her husband would visit the girl's vagina, then come back to bed since Sexy Redd liked to sleep alone. Lisa would have to take care of herself just like she did before she got married.

"Just stay, please!" Lisa said as she reached her breaking point. She felt things were as bad as they could get, so she begged her husband to stay with her.

"I'll be back," he said and stepped out the room. The plush carpet muted his footsteps, but she could hear him tap on her daughter's door.

"Come in!" Sexy Redd called out from the center of her bed. She sat Indian style, making circles on her clit so her box would be hot and ready when company came.

"You ready for this dick?" Jalil asked and peeled off the silk underwear his wife recently bought him.

"I'm always ready for some dick!" she said and fell back with her legs in the air. Jalil was in such a hurry to jump inside the beat up box, he didn't even close the door completely.

Sexy Redd was a sexy motherfucker on the outside but ruined on the inside. He fell straight to the bottom of her vagina as soon as he entered. It was warm and comfy like an old beat up pair of slippers. He began swinging his hips and slinging that dick.

"Awe, man!" Lisa moaned when the sounds of sex seeped down the hall and into her room. Him pounding the soppy vagina sounded like someone running down the hall in flip flops.

She let out a deep sigh and reached over into her nightstand so she could relieve herself. She moved the unused birth control pills that she stopped taking since she wanted to give Jalil a child. If she bore his baby, he would leave her baby and focus on her.

She pushed aside the trusty old 38 she bought for protection and kept looking. Her lonely vagina gave a throb like a puppy wagging its tail when she gripped her faithful vibrator. It always turned her on just to turn it on, especially since it always got her off. Not tonight though. "Awe, man!" she moaned when a twist on the knob did nothing. She found the source of the problem when she realized her husband borrowed the batteries for his video game controller.

There would be no getting off for her tonight. Instead, she had to listen to her daughter and husband go five rounds before sleep saved her from her misery.

CHAPTER 2

Lisa was a broken woman with a broken spirit. She worked doubles and triples once again to avoid the uncomfortable environment in her home. Jalil and Sxy Redd would laugh and talk, only to go silent whenever she entered the room. Like she was interrupting them. She was a stranger in her own house so she hid away at work.

Church was another refuge for her so she would attend every service, class and gathering they offered. Jalil used to accompany her but now stayed home with her daughter. Stayed up in her daughter while she prayed that he wouldn't.

Lisa also prayed for a child. Another child, other than the nasty, foulmouthed woman occupying her home and husband. It would take a miracle since Jalil wouldn't touch her. Miracles do happen though so she kept praying for one. A baby would fix her failed marriage and allow her to have her husband to herself.

"You wanna come to church with me? We can stop at the buffet when service lets out?"' Lisa asked hopefully. She knew how much he enjoyed eating all he could eat at the all you can eat buffet line. It was an ambush so pastor could counsel the couple and save their union. She also knew to whisper so that mean girl running around wouldn't hear.

We haven't been to the buffet in a minute, Jalil thought. It was almost worth sitting through a few hours of pastor what's his name talking about God, or something. Sexy Redd certainly couldn't afford to take him since the only money she had was from the allowance his wife gave him.

"Yup, and they have crab legs! All you can eat!" Lisa sang since that should do the trick. Except she sang a little too loud and the trick heard her.

"Bitch I got all he need to eat right here!" Sexy Redd shouted and patted her box through the tiny shorts she wore around the house.

Lisa reeled at the revelation of her husband going down on the woman since he never went down on her. She looked to him to deny it but he just confirmed it by blinking sheepishly.

"I'm telling pastor!" she shouted at the both of them and rushed from the room. Not before the dry cackle of her daughter's laugh assaulted her ears. The humorless laugh reverberated around her thoughts as she sped to the church. She could even hear it still ringing in the back of her mind as preacher preached about whatever he was preaching about. Most of it was missed by Lisa due to the sting, and ring of her daughter laughing at her.

Well, Lisa punked out after the service and didn't get in the long line to speak to the preacher. Instead, she beat the long line at the buffet and reflected about the sermon over her salad.

Lisa took the long way home since she dreaded being there. Especially after getting laughed at when she left.

Lisa let out a deep sigh when she pulled up into her driveway like a battered husband who hates to come home to face a combative wife. The smell of BBQ lingered in the air and made her glad she only picked over a salad at the buffet. She had a couple thick T-bone steaks marinating for later.

"Smoked in my damn house again," Lisa grumbled to herself when she walked into her smoke filled house. Jalil used to smoke his weed and menthols on the deck until Sexy Redd came home. Now they would smoke all over her house as if they paid the bills and made the rules.

She followed the howling laughter into the den and found the couple cuddled up on the sofa. As usual, they went silent and glared at the intrusion. Lisa frowned at the empty plates on the table. Only the T of the T-bones were left behind.

"You cooked my steak?" she asked with her face twisted in confusion. It was like someone was speaking a foreign language to think he cooked her food and didn't save her any.

"Don't be worried about all dat!" Sexy Redd demanded in defense of her man. "We got bigger thangs to talk 'bout. Tell her, bae."

"Um, well. Okay, see," Jalil stammered and stumbled over his words.

"Soft ass nigga!" the girl giggled and spoke up for him. "Look, he done knocked me up. So, it ain't right for y'all to stay married, since he finna be my baby daddy."

Lisa just blinked as the strange words processed in her head. First, she deciphered the ghetto slang but it still didn't make much sense. Then, she was supposed to get pregnant by her husband. Not her daughter.

"You're not pregnant by my husband," Lisa lifted her chin and proclaimed. Her blood began to slowly boil like a teakettle does before it blows.

"Yes I'm is! So y'all gotta get a divorce!" she demanded once more. Lisa remembered the pregnancy test she had bought when she hoped her husband would get her pregnant. She kept it in the same drawer as her trusty 38, birth control, and vibrtor.

"We're about to see!" Lisa decided and turned to retrieve the test. Either way she had, had enough. To make matters worse, her daughter laughed at her again as she stomped away. That same dry, humorless cackle that stung way down to her soul.

"Her fat ass big mad! Ha ha ha," Sexy Redd sang as her mother went to get the pregnancy test. She was still laughing when she returned. Laughing so hard, she didn't see the gun in her mother's hand. Jalil did and jumped up to protect his woman.

"Hole up now!" Jalil snapped a stepped in front of Sexy Redd like he was bullet proof. He wasn't though and one tug on the trigger ended his part of this story.

"They shooting!" Sexy Redd shouted and took off running. Tried to anyway that is as another tug dropped her before she got too far. The slug tore through her spine and permanently paralyzed her. She would never twerk or even walk again for the rest of her life. That wasn't very long though because the laughter still rung in Lisa's ears louder than the gunshots.

"Ha ha this! And this and this!" Lisa said and punctuated each "this" with a 38 caliber punctuation mark.

"Oh and you," Lisa said and she turned back to the shell her husband once lived in. He had moved out from the first shot but she still put the gun to his temple and fired once more. "I divorce you!"

*****

"Uh oh!" Lisa giggled when she came back from blacking out. An hour had past and her family lay stiff and cold around the room. The lingering smell of gunpowder mixed with the coppery smell of spilt blood.

"My ass is in trouble," she realized as she surveyed the carnage. Her mind raced and chased different excuses and explanations. In the end, she decided to lie.

She used the butt of the gun to break one of the windowpanes to make it look like a burglary gone wrong. She tilted over a few items and opened a few drawers. The murder weapon had to go so she put it back in a different drawer and hid it under her panties.

A growl from her stomach helped with an alibi, so she went out to grab something to eat. She was in the mood for steak and headed over to Ruth Chris for a T-bone.

Hours had past by the time she returned and it was show time. She called 911 and reported finding her family dead in the den. The operator advised her to not to touch anyone or anything and wait outside. That's where she was when the first of what would be many police cars arrived.

"Is anyone still in there?" the patrol officer asked as he got out.

"I don't think so?" Lisa lied. The cop pulled his weapon and went inside to clear the house just like the cops on the cop shows.

"Clear!" he called out to no one as he went room to room. Until he reached that room with the dead people sprawled around.

Soon the subdivision was buzzing with officials and officially nosey neighbors. People peeked out blinds or posted up on porches to see what was going on in a neighborhood where nothing was ever going on.

"Mrs. Robinson?" a detective asked as he approached Lisa in the driveway. The question seemed to confuse her since she wasn't sure if she should or even could still use her married name since she obviously wasn't married anymore.

"Um, yes?" she decided.

"Can you tell me what happened?" he asked softly since she had just lost her family.

"They got killed," Lisa nodded and stopped like that was the end of her story.

"Did your husband or daughter have any enemies? Where they threatened?" he asked in search of a motive for the madness.

"Just me," she giggled and caught herself. It warmed her heart that they paid for their indiscretion and disrespect. The detective was used to strange reactions from people in shock, but this was the strangest yet.

"I'll have an officer transport you to the station so we can take a formal statement," he decided and waved a uniformed officer over.

"Can we do it next week? That would be better for me," Lisa said. Her request as denied and she was escorted to a cop car. She got to ride up front this time, but it would be the last time if she didn't get her story straight.

"Look it, sarge!" another detective said and pointed at the security cameras around the house. One at the front door, one at the back door and one in the den.

"Call the company and have to footage sent to the office," he said. He continued on and examined the scene. He'd been doing this long enough to know this was personal. People get gunned down all the time during burglaries, but not like this. Lisa's story had more holes in it than her daughter.

"Any shell casings?" he asked as he looked around himself for spent cartridges.

"Not a one. Must have been a revolver. Who has time to police their brass during a break in?" the younger cop asked. The sergeant nodded along with his correct reasoning.

"Sarge!" another cop called from upstairs. The lead detective turned and followed his voice to the master bedroom. The cop pointed to the open drawer where the 38 was waiting to be found.

"Recently fired," he said from the smell of fresh powder emanating up from the drawer.

"I'll bag it and tag it," he said and did just that. The sergeant had seen all he needed to see and left his subordinates to wrap up the crime scene. He headed over to the station to interview a killer.

CHAPTER 3

Lisa had been left alone in an interrogation room to stew for a few hours before the lead detective came in to see her. She used the time wisely and concocted a good story to tell them. When he finally came in she was ready, but so was he.

"I'm sorry to keep you waiting. I had to review some video. Sorry for your loss," he said and studied her reaction.

"Thank you," she said and wiped away an invisible tear.

"I'm Detective Black. I'll be handling this case," he said and sat his laptop on the table between them. He positioned the screen so they both could see it and continued. The law required a Miranda warning, so he gave it and began. "Tell me again what happened?"

"Well, I went to church. The preacher was talking about God and stuff and..." she said as he began the video. Her head tilted as she saw her den pop up on the screen. She wondered if it was a live feed until she saw the dead people.

"Is that your late husband?" he asked and pointed to Jalil stretched out on the sofa.

"Uh, yes," she agreed as her daughter came in the room in one of her stripper outfits.

"And I assume that's your daughter?" he asked as she began to twerk up a storm.

The room went quiet as the sound of Sexy Redd's clapping cheeks filled the air. It was bad but got worse when Jalil pulled her down on the sofa and dipped his face between the tatted up thighs. He ignored the different names on each leg and ate out the middle.

"I had zero interest on that sofa," Lisa remarked. She finally had an answer to the recent stains on the fabric when her husband fucked her daughter right there on the spot. The video continued and they both ate steaks after the sex, then smoked a blunt.

"And who is this?" detective Black asked when Lisa came into the picture.

"Um," she said and watched herself murder her family on the video. "I probably need a lawyer?"

"Lady, you're going to need a shovel. So you can go dig Johnnie Cochran up," the cop said and stood. He opened the door and let in a uniformed officer to take her over to the jail. An open and shut case if ever there was one.

"Turn around. Hands behind your back," the cop said and put handcuffs on the woman for the first time in her life.

Lisa had a blank stare with the occasional blink as she was taken to the jail. The process was a blur of pictures, prints, strip search, and uniforms. She was given a net bag filled with the things needed for her stay.

"Why?" she wanted to know when she told to squat and cough. The words were still in the air when the woman next to her complied to the command. She got her answer when a crack pipe fell out of her. The beat up box had lost all of its grip many miles away. A crack heads vagina can rack up more mile than a New York city taxi cab.

"One more!" the officer demanded and twisted her lips skeptically.

"Awe, man," the woman moaned and repeated the process and produced a lighter and couple bags of crack.

Lisa squatted and coughed but didn't produce any contraband

*****

Hours later, Lisa and the crack head were taken up to the dorm that would be their home until the courts said otherwise. The large day room was loud and shrill from thirty-six screaming women. They screamed at the TV, at each other across the spades game, or just screamed to be screaming.

The noise was one thing, but the smell took her by surprise. Thirty-four vaginas in an enclosed area with poor circulation present obvious challenges, but it was more than that. It was a strange aroma she had never experienced before. A mix of broken dreams, ash of burned bridges and fear.

"You got a new roommate, Kisha!" a girl called out since that room had an empty bunk.

"Who!" Kisha barked in an attempt to sound tough, but most of the fear in the room emanated from her pores. She got her answer when Lisa acknowledged the number over the cell door as the same on her wristband. She let out a deep sigh and ventured inside.

"Awe, man!" another girl moaned when that left the crack head to be her bunkmate. "Know her ole ass smell like fish!"

"Holy mackerel, bat girl!" Shay laughed. She was the roughest, toughest stud in the dorm, so everyone laughed when she laughed. Meanwhile, Kisha went to investigate her new bunkmate.

"Sup, auntie? I'm Kisha," Kisha greeted while checking her net bag for anything she could get out of her. They could tell in an instant that Lisa wasn't from the streets.

"Um, Lisa," she replied as the girl gave her a once over and left.

"What she talmbout?" Shay wanted to know.

"She square as fuck. Need to pay rent 'round here!" Kisha said. The women who couldn't fight or weren't affiliated had to pay to stay.

"She bout to be!" Shay laughed. "We finna press up on her ass after chow!"

Lisa used the thin sheet and course blanket to make her mat similar to the diagram on the wall. She had to step on the stool built on to the built-in desk mounted on the wall. It wasn't easy, but she managed to make it happen. The events of the day pulled her up on the bunk and rocked her to sleep.

"Chow, auntie! Chicken on the bone!" another young girl announced and knocked. She wore the glee and excitement that the once every two-weeks delicacy brings. It was the only piece of real meat the massive jail served.

"Huh?" Lisa asked from the confusion of being woke from her nap—her strange environment and the stranger.

"Chow! Hurry up! They finna close the door!" she urged. Lisa didn't quite get what she was saying, but the sense of urgency prompted her to move.

Lisa came out just as the officer came through and shut the doors. She seemed disappointed that she wasn't able to prevent anyone from eating.

The rat pack cut the line of women lining up for their dinner trays. They looked in faces to see if anyone had a problem with it. That would give them a reason to fight and take their chicken. No one did, so they watched Lisa fall into the back of the line.

"News on!" an older woman shouted to alert the dorm. The young girls ran the TV, but gave the rest an hour for the nightly news. The rest of the day, it was tuned into the buffoonery that they loved. The unrealistic reality that led to their reality of being in jail.

In the top stories tonight, a mother has been arrested and charged with the double murder of her own daughter and husband...

All heads turned and lifted upwards towards the TV at the mention of the heinous crime. Even Lisa turned to see who was ruthless enough to spill the blood of their blood. There were plenty of women in here for stabbing or shooting husbands and boyfriends, but killing your own kid is another level.

The mood in the dorm shifted as quickly as spring in Georgia. Lisa was embarrassed when she heard the heinous crime along with her mugshot on the screen. She had no idea it just saved her from more problems than she could handle. No worries though since she had plenty more problems still to come.

CHAPTER 3

"Hey, auntie? They calling you!" Kisha called out as she rushed into the cell they shared. The young girls now looked up to her since she was a killer and all. Had she been a teacher or nurse, she would have lost some weight by now because they wouldn't let her eat.

"Me?" Lisa asked and pointed at herself for confirmation. She had been in her bunk for the three days since being arrested. Mainly under the course blanket hiding from her reality. The double homicide was still top news until a better murder came along. Lucky for her, one was in the works.

"Yeah, you got a visit!" the girl cheered. She never had a visit herself, so she was happy someone she knew got one.

She, like the rest of the rat pack, never got money on the books or visits. Even if a family member wanted to come, the girls had long burned their bridges behind them so no one could get across.

Lisa hadn't called anyone since getting arrested, so she wondered who while washing the signs of sleep off of her face. She only had three people in her life that it could be. She reduced it to two when she killed her daughter. Now, it could only be the wayward man who fathered her child or the woman who birthed her way back when.

Then was the needy mother who only came around when she needed something. Lisa raised her part-time since she always needed a loan or "a lil help". They had been estranged lately since all of Lisa's lil help went towards her deadbeat husband.

Lisa was still wondering which of the two it could be when she came out of the dorm. Both options came with a big why until she remembered why she was here. Defending her actions in court was one thing, now she had to answer to her family.

"Mama," she said when she saw her own mother on the other side of the inch thick plexiglass. She sat down and they both began talking at the same time. Neither had been here before, so neither picked up the receiver to be heard.

"The phone, baby," her mother and caught on when she saw a veteran girl beside her talk to her friend. They both lifted the phone to their mouths and spoke again. "Please tell me you didn't kill Lenika, my grandbaby."

Lisa lowered her head in shame when she heard the anguish in her voice. Her justifications went out the window since she couldn't she explain killing her own child to her own mother.

"They were sleeping together. In my own house, while I was hard at work taking care of them both," she said under her breath. Now, days later it didn't sound like it was punishable by death. Her mother's head shook from side to side, but she still didn't side with her.

"So, you kill her? Him, I get. But your daughter? Oh, baby. How could you?" she asked and drowned out any chance to answer with her tears and wails. Five of the allotted thirty minutes were gone by the time she simmered down.

"My baby!" Lisa moaned as the reality crashed down like a ton of bricks. All she could see now was the pretty, yellow baby she gave birth to. Gone was the ratchet hood rat she grew up to be.

"What are they saying? Can you come home?" her mother asked.

"I'm pretty sure I can't. I'm going to need a lawyer," Lisa surmised.

"Lawyers are expensive! I can't afford no lawyer!" the woman wailed. Lisa pondered for a moment before nodding with her own decision.

"I have savings. Should be more than enough," she said of her savings and 401k. Not to mention her home was paid off which gave her even more

"Tell me what you need me to do?" her mother asked eagerly. All the distance between seemed to vanish in an instant. There was something else in her eye, but Lisa didn't know what to make of it. She was desperate and ready to accept any help she could get.

"I'll have to give you power of attorney. This will allow you access to the funds to pay a lawyer," she explained. She saw a twinkle in her mother's eye that gave her hope. The woman may not have been there much in her life, but she was here now.

The thirty minutes ticked off quickly and it was time to go. Mother and daughter touched the glass and said goodbye for now. The mother returned the next day with the legal documents that granted her power of attorney and access to everything Lisa worked hard for.

*****

"Power of attorney? I'on know nothing about no power of attorney!" Patricia grumbled to herself as she entered the bank. The woman never had an account of her own since she never had anything to put in it.

Whatever money she had was tucked away in a bible or her bosom. Only until she had a chance to play her numbers or a little tonk with her friends. Those same friends were on their way to Biloxi this weekend, but she didn't have the money to go with them. She did, but tried to flip it playing scratch-offs so she would have more to gamble with. It didn't pay off, so she only played herself. Especially when she asked her daughter for the money and got shot down.

"May I help you?" a banker asked when she peeped the perplexed woman standing in the middle of the bank.

"I'm supposed to be some kind of lawyer," Patrica advised and passed her the document.

"Oooh!" the lady said and smiled when she read the power of attorney forms. She led her to her desk and pulled up the account. "So what are you trying to do?"

"Well, I have to give some money to my daughter's lawyer. Pay some bills, insurance..." she read from her list.

Here we go again, the banker thought to herself. She had seen incapacitated people give inexperienced people power of attorney to help them out in a jam, only to end up in a worse jam. In her twenty years, it never came out well. Even if off by only a dollar, it never turned out right.

"Okay, we can get you some cashiers checks to cover the bills," she offered. The strange words furrowed her brow even more. "Or money orders, I guess."

"Cash in best," Patricia nodded since they were back to speaking English.

"Okay, let's total this," she said and took the paper from her hand. Her eyes went wide at the thirty thousand notation for a lawyer. "We have to close an IRA for the lawyer fee. You'll have to come back on Monday."

"How much money is in there?" the mother asked and craned her neck for a look. She soon got wide eyed when she saw all those zeros. Patricia had a combined total of one hundred thousand dollars. Most was in IRAs and CDs. Another twenty-five grand was spread over checking and savings.

All Patricia could think of at the moment was getting turned down for five hundred to go gamble with her friends. She promised to pay it back when they returned on Monday, but Lisa wouldn't budge. She said she didn't have money for that, but all her mother heard was she didn't have money.

"Hmph. So, l can take out five hundred now?" Patricia asked and looked at the clock to see if she could still make the bus.

"Um, sure," the banker sighed. The woman had power of attorney and could take out whatever she wanted.

"How about a thousand then?" she asked with her head tilted like a dare. The banker could only nod since angels record every word uttered. She didn't want to see that word again when she met her Lord or be a party to it now.

"Just fill out a withdrawal form and take it to a teller," she advised. She watched the woman do just that and approach the teller. Patricia got her cash and rushed from the bank as swiftly as a robber does. Curiosity got the best of her, so she picked up her receiver and hit the teller on hers.

"Hey, Carol," the teller greeted and waved across the bank to her.

"Hey, Chardonnay," she replied and paused so she wouldn't giggle at her name. "Tell me, how much did that woman withdraw?"

"Five thousand dollars. She said she was putting it back on Monday," she replied of the strange transaction. Carol just shook her head and placed the receiver back on its cradle. These things never turn out well.

CHAPTER 4

"Hmph!" Patricia said to on no one as she nestled into the comfy first class seat. She may have missed the bus with her friends, but the flight would get her there before them.

A couple hours and couple drinks later, she was in the Gulfport for some good gambling. Both intoxicants and gambling are abominations of the devil's handiwork, so even if you win, you still lose.

"Hmph!" she said once more when she had a choice between an Uber or a limo. The limo pulled up in perfect time for her friends to see her get out.

"Patricia!" Maggie shrieked when she saw her. She had been planning on rubbing the trip in her face when she got back.

"Yes, it's me!" Patricia said and left off the "bitches" on the tip of her tongue. She lifted her head and led the ladies inside. Most of these bus rides didn't include a room, so the woman stayed in the casino until it was time to go home.

"Well, I'm fixing to throw these bones!" Athea declared and made a beeline to the dice table.

"Black jack for me," Maggie announced and spun on her heels. Patricia was a slots girl herself and headed over to pull on the one armed bandits. There's a reason they were called that but none of the hundred people tugging on the levers got that memo.

"You look like the one!" Patricia decided when she picked out a slot machine. She usually spent the whole twenty-four hours on the same machine. She greeted the woman on the next machine with a nod.

"This bitch is ready to pay out!" the woman insisted with each pull of the arm. The machine robbed her of every token she put in it.

"You the one, ain't you?" Patricia purred and rubbed the machine like she did her cat. It had a ten thousand dollar pay out, and she could put it back on Monday. Then handle the bills her daughter asked her to handle.

The two similar women made similar small talk as they fed dollar tokens into the machine. Both came from failed marriages and estranged children. Both took turns paying for drinks to keep lubricated so they could pull on the machines.

"So deacon and sister..." the woman began but paused when a second cherry matched the first. One more cherry and, "Jackpot!"

"Shit!" Patricia fussed at the woman striking gold before she did. It too had a ten thousand dollar pay out and produced a golden ticket to be redeemed at their cashier's cage. The cage took in way more money than it took in and she had plans for her winnings.

"I'm finna go buy me some!" she proclaimed like she had hit the jackpot again.

"Huh?" Patricia asked since she had never heard of such a thing.

"Girl, what you think them dudes hanging out in the bar is for?" she explained.

"Huh?" she asked again as she looked over to see what the woman was talking about.

She did see plenty of younger men posted up with older woman. Dudes who preyed on the lonely churches ladies who came down for weekend getaways. Their husbands never knew why they never came home with any winnings. They won plenty but traded it for some dick before they got home.

The woman she was talking to rushed off and cashed out her ticket. She hobbled into the bar and came out a few minutes later with a pretty boy that was half her age. They went straight to the bank of elevators and headed up to her room.

"Hmph," Patricia wondered about the prospect of buying some dick. It had been a while since she had some. The last time she got laid was to some old player she'd met at the local American Legion. She had to wait an hour for his little purple pill to raise up his brown dick. It was mediocre at best and it left her unfulfilled. She absent-mindedly pulled on the slot machine while admiring the gigolos in the bar.

"Un uh!" she denied and shook her head when she saw Maggie hustle into the elevator with a young, high yellow fellow. Her husband was banging everything in sight back home, so he always sent her off on these trips. Little did he know, she was purchasing some penis while she was here.

A minor jackpot sounded the alarm on Patricia's machine. It was only five hundred of the thousands it had taken in for the day, but it was enough.

"Hmph!" she announced and decided it was enough to buy her some dick too. She slid off the stool and tossed the rest of her drink down her the throat. Someone slid on the machine before she took two steps away. After cashing out her ticket, she entered the bar to pick out some dick.

"Hey, beautiful lady," a handsome guy with an athletic build said and showed off his new smile. His once crooked teeth where now straight courtesy of the curved dick in his gifted silk drawers.

"Hey, yourself," Patricia said and paused to give him a once over. Her lips pursed into a scrupulous pucker as she checked him out from head to toe. He looked clean and wore size eleven shoes, but that could be deceptive. She may have been spending someone else's money but still wanted the most for it. Not too much though, since it had been a while.

"This what you wondering about?" he asked and pulled her hand onto his meat. She gave it a squeeze as if selecting a melon.

"Oh, chile!" she snickered and pulled away. The man was around the age of the granddaughter she had just lost, but this wasn't the time for mourning.

"So, you trying to spend a little time?" he asked. He said time but meant money because time is money in his line of work. The trick was doing numbers. The more old ladies he ran through, the more money he made.

"How much?" she said like a dare. That meant "yes" in his world, so it was his turn to scrutinize her for her worth and wealth.

"Gimme two hundred," he decided. He could see she was one of the bus riders and hit her up for a reasonable price. Her old lady blouse and sensible shoes said she couldn't stand much more than that.

"Come on!" Patricia agreed and dragged him towards the elevator. The gigolos kept rooms on standby for a kickback to the desk.

"I'm Carlton," he introduced as they rode up to his room.

"Patricia," she said warmly and grinned in anticipation. Carlton grinned too since he could tell she hadn't had any dick in a while. Even the married ones went months without some dick and were powder kegs ready to blow by the time they took a trip down to Biloxi.

He especially liked the church groups since he got triple the rewards when he went up in them. First, those old ladies had some good pussy. Spent well and gave a mini sermon when he got them off. They would "yes lawd" and "oh gawd" the whole time. Then pray for him with a "bless this chile" once they got their rocks off.

"After you," Carlton said as he used the key card to open the door. Patricia hadn't been treated like a lady in never, so she giggled again at the chivalry.

"Let me get you your money!" she declared and opened her purse to pay him before he got away. She was too eager and missed the greed that flashed in his eyes when he saw the roll of cash.

"You ain't trying to get any extras, are you?" he asked in search of more of her money.

"Extras?" she asked with a twinkle in her eyes. "What extras?"

"Eat the pussy, a hundred. Back shots, seventy-five. Riding..." he said and ran down the add-on menu. By the time they climbed in the bed, she had spent another three hundred dollars.

"Whew, child!" Patricia proclaimed when Carlton beat her back out one last time. That was Monday morning and it was time to head back to Atlanta. She hadn't stepped foot back in the casino since she left. She did hit the 24-hour teller a few times and spent a few grand on the young man. He would have stayed there for as long as she liked as long as she was spending.

"I can go again if you want?" Carlton asked and paused. Orgasms were extra too, so the meter stopped once she stopped shivering and shaking from this one. She would have to put some more coins in the meter to get his hips going again.

"Chile, I gotta catch a flight. I got to get back to Atlanta!" she sighed.

"Next time then," he shrugged and took the dick away. Not without a fight though since she had gotten hooked on it.

"Why don't you come?" she heard herself say. It was already out, so she nodded and doubled down. "I got more money a

Carlton called his girlfriend and let her know he would be gone for a while. She was cool as he brought that money back. He flew first class and laid some first class pipe for almost two months.

Patricia fed him, clothed him, iced him, and even brought things for his sister and mother who was really his girlfriend at home. Carlton put the dick down so good, she treated him to a brand new car, as well. Two months later, the river of cash dwindled to a trickle after she tricked off almost a hundred grand on dick.

Once the well went dry, he fucked the old lady into a coma and loaded his new Dodge Charger with his loot. By the time she awoke from the dick induced slumber, he was back home in Mississippi.

"Uh oh!" Patricia said when she finally came to her senses. She had ignored the letters her daughter had sent from the jail through indigent postage since she knew what she wanted. She did decide to open up one of the letters from the bank in case there was a few bucks left that she somehow overlooked.

"Jackpot!" Patricia cheered when she saw the offer to use equity in the home. It specified home improvements or college funds but neither pertained to her. She had a better idea what to do with the money.

"I'll fly out to Vegas and double it!" she decided. Instead, she flew out first class and had to take the bus back when she lost every penny.

CHAPTER 5

"What's wrong with you, auntie?" Kisha asked when she saw Lisa's face go white when she read her mail. The woman expected bad, but hoped for the best when she didn't hear back from her mother. She was hoping the woman had died and her money was safe. The letter from the bank had killed those hopes as dead as her daughter was.

"I, I, I," was all that would come out since she forget how to speak at the moment. She just handed the letter over so she could see for herself.

"Dang!" the girl fussed when she saw the bill. She didn't know the legal mumble jumble any better than Patricia did, but recognized the number. "How you owe them that much money?"

"I have no idea," she moaned and tried to make sense of it. Not only had her mother spent every penny she had, but she lost her house and over drafted all of her accounts. Patricia went right back to being broke and was cool with it. It was bad for Lisa but was about to get worse.

"So, if you don't get your money for your lawyer, you gone have to use a public pretender!" Kisha gasped. She had been in and out of jail long enough to know the public defenders office couldn't get a ham sandwich off for killing Tupac.

"Yeah, I know," Lisa said and drifted into a funk. A dangerous dive of depression and despair.

The woman was already losing weight from the county jail cuisine but now paced constantly during the day. She added push ups and sit ups to her routine to keep her mind off of her upcoming trial. By the time her court date rolled around, she was two hundred pounds of breast and muscles.

*****

"Don't worry, auntie. You gonna be just fine!" Kisha said when Lisa was called out for court.

"No she ain't. They finna give her the needle!" Shay laughed. It was real funny until Lisa stopped and gave her a deadly glare. When Shay stopped smiling, she resumed walking and left the dorm.

"I don't think I have court today. I still haven't seen my lawyer," Lisa said. She had gotten a letter from the public defenders office with a name but nothing more.

"Tell it to the judge," the officer shrugged. She heard shit every day that she didn't care about and couldn't solve if she did. Her job was to open doors, count inmates, and not die.

Lisa tuned out the chatter on the bus as they rode over to the court. The few female inmates were segregated by a wire partition from the guys. Close enough to see, smell and hear, but not touch.

"Let us see something, auntie!" one of the young men asked as they rode. All the other girls were flashing tits while the guys pulled on their dks. Most were facing a lifetime of time ahead of them in court, but they wanted to get off before they got there.

Lisa sighed and stared straight ahead while the rest of the people partied like it was a party bus instead of life or death that awaited in the courthouse. The women were let off first and taken into a separate holding tank until their case was called.

"Robinson, Lisa!" a deputy asked as he opened the cell.

"That's me!" she said and stood. Lisa followed her to another cell where a change of clothes awaited. The court provided a nice, used business suit except it was the size she used to be instead of the size she currently was.

"You ready?" the deputy asked when he answered Lisa's tap on the door.

"Yes, no. These don't fit," she said and raised her hands so he could see the clothes hanging off. He gave a "not my problem" shrug and cuffed her once more for the elevator ride to the courtroom.

"Over there," her escort said and pointed to the defense table. She frowned curiously at the disheveled white man seated. He multitasked by reading a file and picking his nose at the same time.

"Lisha?" the man asked and offered the same hand he just used to pick his nose. He wondered why she scrunched her face up at it until he looked down and saw the green booger on the tip. He wiped it on his wrinkled suite and tried again. "I'm Daryl King, your lawyer."

"It's Lisa and 'bout dang time!" she fussed and took the seat beside him.

"I was just assigned your case this morning," he said and licked his booger finger and flipped a page.

"So, when am I supposed to go to trial? They're going to postpone it, I'm sure?" she asked as the room began to fill.

"All rise!" a bailiff announced and the white haired judge stepped from his chambers.

"Uh, right now!" King said and scrambled to his feet, while still trying to read her case file.

"In the case of the state of Georgia verses Lisa Robinson. Are both sides ready to proceed for trial?" the ancient judge asked and peered down at both tables.

"Ready, your Honor!" a spunky assistant district attorney nearly cheered. He had been up for weeks preparing his case. All of his ducks were in a row and he was ready to go. The courtroom went silent and all eyes shifted over to the defense table.

"Uh, I think they want you," Lisa said unsurely.

"Is the defense ready for trial?" the judge asked again.

"Ready as I'm going to be!" King said with a chuckle. No one else thought anything was funny, especially his client. Even the prosecutor shook his head at the ineffective counsel.

Lisa mainly blinked and winced as the state laid out its case against her. She even sounded guilty to herself. Her lawyer objected to nothing and silently took it all in since he only read a few pages into the case file.

The jury looked sympathetic of her plight until the medical examiner testified about the injuries and overkill.

"I'm done," Lisa admitted when they showed the surveillance video of her gunning her family down.

"Yeah," he lawyer admitted with another chuckle. He had no questions for any of the state's witnesses and had no witnesses of his own to call. After all, he just got the case that morning. By that afternoon, it was time for closing arguments before the case went to the jury.

"Ladies and gentlemen, the law is clear. You can't kill people," the prosecutor began. He played the video one last time and dropped the mic.

"A bit dramatic, don't you think?" the judge admonished and looked to the defense table.

"Uh, oh ok," Mr. King said and stood. "No, you can't kill people. We agree on that, but this wasn't murder. This was the result of a sudden rage, inflamed passion. And according to the laws of this state, that's manslaughter."

The assistant district attorney's eyes went wide when he heard the truth. The judge very well should have instructed on manslaughter charges at that point. Luckily for the state, the judge had nodded off for a moment. His clerk pulled the string attached to his robe to wake him up.

The jury was sent to the deliberation room to deliberate even though their minds were made up. Most didn't even sit when they reached the room. The word "guilty" reverberated around the room on all charges. They alerted the bailiff and were escorted back to the courtroom.

"Uh oh," King mumbled when the news of the quick verdict was announced. He hoped to have time to use the bathroom and eat his lunch before they found his client guilty. He didn't, so he opened his sandwich and scarfed it down while taking a dump.

Once all parties were reunited in the courtroom, the foreman passed the judge the verdict. He nodded at it and sent it back for the formal reading.

"As to count one, murder. How does the jury find?" he asked even though he knew.

"Guilty!" the foreman announced. He repeated himself on another count of murder. Two counts of felony murder, two aggravated assaults, and a host of other charges the state added to stack the deck.

"I hereby sentence you to death by lethal inject—" the judge began until he felt a tug on his string.

"This wasn't a death penalty case," the prosecutor said and sighed. Every prosecutor wants to put a defendant on death row and this would have been his shot had his boss approved it.

"My bad," the judge corrected and gave the correct sentence. "Life, life, twenty years, ten years..."

Lisa just blinked in disbelief as she was sentenced to "from now on" in the penitentiary.

"Sorry, Lisha," King said but ruined the apology with a shoulder shrug.

She was in a dazed state of suspended animation for the rest of the day. It still didn't register when she was taken back to the holding cell to change out of the borrowed clothing. Nor when she was chained and shackled for the bus ride back to the prison.

Those same rowdy dudes had lost some of that energy they had on the ride over. Most were going to prison too and that was nothing to celebrate. No one wanted to see anything or pull on themselves now.

"So, how it went?" a girl asked when Lisa slinked into the dorm.

"Life, life and like sixty years," she croaked and sucked all the air out of the large room. Most had pending charges and this could very well be their outcome, as well.

"Tole you her ass was getting life! Ha ha, ha ha!" Shay teased. For the first time, she couldn't get anyone to laugh along with her, but that didn't stop her from mocking the woman.

Lisa did her best to tune the clown out, but she kept on clowning. For the next hour, she talked the TV to tease the woman. She only paused when the case was on the news.

"An Atlanta woman was sentence to two life sentences and sixty years for the murder of her husband and daughter..." the reporter reported.

"Ha ha, ha ha," Shay grunted nonstop. She wouldn't even let up when the dinner trays came in. She even snatched Lisa's chicken on the bone off the thick plastic tray and sat down.

Lisa stared down at what was left on her tray and snarled. She titled it over and let the greens and beans fall to the stainless steel table. Shay was yapping and smacking as Lisa came up behind her. The sudden silence in the never silent dorm alerted her and caused her to look up.

She looked up just in time to see the plastic tray speeding towards her face. The crack of her cheekbone filled the air and knocked her on her ass. Lisa stood over her and beat her unmercifully with the tray. Blood sprayed as bones crushed in her face. She kept on beating until the officers rushed in to stop her.

That was easier said than done since she ignored their verbal commands. Next came the pepper spray, but it had no affect on the woman. The beating only stopped when the tray was crushed and useless.

"Gimme my damn chicken!" she fussed and ate it off the bone.

Lisa was already going to prison, so now she was headed to D-block.

Hood Chronicles

Born on the west side of Chicago, Hood Chronicles found himself conditioned to the violence surrounding him at an early age. Indulging in a thug's life, as a former drug dealer, weapons trafficker, and convicted felon, he realized that he could no longer follow the footsteps of deception. He soon found a better path to tread in the literary world.

After witnessing abuse, domestic violence, and murder, his mother decided to relocate down south to Georgia. College Park may have been a breath of fresh air to her, but for him, his new home on Godby Road presented the same horrific sights as the Illinois streets.

Coming of age, Hood found himself dabbling in the drug trade in order to earn extra money. Things were going well until he found a crack head's knife at his teenage throat. Robbed of all of his money and drugs, Hood vowed to never leave himself vulnerable again. With a newfound passion for guns, he couldn't avoid the violence in which his mother attempted to save him from.

Categorized as a menace to society by the Atlanta Police department, Hood became imprisoned as a child for the offense of murder. What appeared to be a curse, eventually became his precious gift. As time passed, maturity developed and a new purpose in life was born.

Facing the death penalty, Hood Chronicles fought for a lighter sentence that would grant him some type of opportunity to rectify his ways. While incarcerated, he began to write about his life in the streets and the pitfalls of reckless conduct. Realizing his talent for the art of storytelling combined with the graphic experiences of a hustler's ambition, Hood quickly took notice of his way out of the Trap.

Transitioning from a thug, to a revered voice in the literary world, Hood Chronicles is now more focused than ever. As one of the most prolific and diverse Urban lit authors of this age, Hood challenges you to enter into his creative world of danger, suspense, eroticism, and all out street grit!

URBAN AESOP PRESENTS

WHORE

HOOD

CHRONICLES

Whore
A Short Story by
Hood Chronicles

Chapter 1

Amber watched as a trick named Lawrence came through her motel room door. She had met him online like she did all of her clientele. Her pimp, King, had a deal with the motel manager. He would pay double the room cost for a few to be serviced by his "working girls". As far as the manager was concerned, half would cover the room fee, while the other half would line the insides of his greedy pockets. All was well for King as long as his hoes did their jobs. Come hell or high water, he was going to make sure that his hoes did their jobs.

Lawrence was a newbie. He weighed in at a whopping 350 pounds and only stood 5'2". Needless to say, he was a short, fat, high-yellow piece of sweaty and undesirable flesh. Amber simply smiled and welcomed him inside.

"I know this is your first time with me, but like I said online, you got to pay before we play," she reminded him.

Lawrence nodded his head in agreement and retrieved his wallet from his pocket. Pulling out three hundred dollars, he placed the bills into Amber's palms. She was now satisfied and all his until climax.

Lawrence watched as she stood before him clad in a hot pink, lace lingerie gown. Underneath it rested nothing more than golden brown skin, perky breasts, and chocolate-coated nipples. Lawrence began to tremble and sweat profusely as she drew near.

"It's okay, baby," she whispered, dropping to her knees to unbuckle his belt.

As she began to loosen his jeans, Lawrence fell back across the bed on his elbows, awaiting what he knew was to come. Reaching inside his boxers, she felt around until she felt his penis.

"What the fuck?" she whispered to no one in particular.

She couldn't believe her eyes as she took a closer look. His dick was damn near the size of a super-sized Tic Tac. She fought back the urge to giggle when the stench of his shitty underwear hit her square in the nostrils. Her mind was racing a million miles per hour, but she knew she had to get that money up for King.

Leaning forward, she began to lick the tip of his manhood. Pleased, Lawrence reached forward and mashed her head down into his greasy lap. Amber began to suck with vigor before she suffocated to death. Surprised, Lawrence was a less than a minuteman. He began to squirt his little nut into her mouth and pump like it was no tomorrow.

Elated that her job was done, Amber raced to the bathroom to spit his love oils into the toilet. After rinsing her mouth out, she prepared to escort Lawrence out of her room.

"Okay, baby. Thanks for a great time," she told him.

Lawrence was confused. "What do you mean?"

"I mean, it's over now, and you got to go."

"Go? I ain't pay you three hundred for that! I paid for head, ass, and pussy, so you got two more tasks to take care of as far as I'm concerned," he spat.

Amber placed her hands on her hips and replied, "You paid for a nut, Mr. Minuteman. And now it's time to go."

Lawrence stood in disbelief.

"Oh, you're not going to go? Do I have to get security in here?"

Lawrence couldn't believe it. He simply pulled his pants up and got himself together. Relieved, Amber walked behind him as they moved towards the door. However, Lawrence wasn't prepared to give up so easily. He was pissed beyond belief.

As she reached down to turn the doorknob, Lawrence threw his elbow back to crack her dead in the eye. It split instantly, causing blood to spill. Amber fell backwards and went completely unconscious. At that moment, Lawrence retrieved his cell phone and began to dial up his friends. He was going to teach this hoe a lesson that she'd never forget.

****

Amber awakened to the blurry sight of at least ten men surrounding her. A burning sensation in her rear was excruciating. She attempted to move, but her hands were tied behind her back. Wondering where she was, she began to scream. At that moment, she found that her mouth was stuffed to full capacity. Lawrence had ripped her attire from her body and stuffed it into her mouth. Also, he called a gang of his close friends to come and help him teach the young girl a lesson.

Amber had been sodomized by four men while she was unconscious. She wished that she had remained knocked out as the men began to mount her again . . . and again . . . and again. Lawrence watched as his friends had their way with Amber. The crazed pervs urinated all over her face, leaving her saturated in cum and blood.

Amber knew that King didn't have any security in place for such a dire emergency. She had lied to Lawrence earlier while trying to get him to leave. The poor girl was forced to watch the men take all of her night's earnings and escape without remorse.

She laid in immense pain awaiting King's arrival. It took him three hours before he finally came to round up his stable and collect dues. Amber was fast asleep as King entered with his girls.

"Oh my God!" Trina exclaimed, rushing to her friend's side.

Rena simply stood beside King with a slight smirk across her face.

"Wake up, baby! Wake up!" Trina called, shaking her friend.

Amber's eyes fluttered open as fright gripped her heart. Relieved to see a familiar face, she then became anxious to get free. Trina, accompanied by a couple of other ladies, quickly untied the knots in the ropes in order to release their "sister".

Rena didn't budge. She couldn't stand Amber. The two had so much in common, they could have been best friends in another lifetime. Yet, in this life, Rena considered Amber her number one nemesis. Both girls were eighteen, came to King fresh out of high school, and shared a background of molestation by close relatives. One would think they could set their differences aside, but Rena wasn't having it. She

knew that the rest of King's hoes were considered old due to strict stan-
dards. By twenty-four, your ass was played out, and most of Kings stable were nearly into their thirties.

Rena was the kitten among the cats within her daddy's litter box,
that was until Trina found Amber. Not only was she young but also
beautiful. Rena felt threatened, and every chance she got to stick it to
Amber, she did.

Helping Amber's bruised body up to her feet, the girls ushered her
over to King. He was a tall, dark, and handsome brother who utilized
his looks and charms to finesse women into "the life". After he had
them captivated, he ruled his hoes with an iron fist.

King studied the puffiness around Amber's eyes and the huge split.
Grasping her chin, he turned her head from right to left.

"Explain," he nonchalantly demanded.

"A trick knocked me unconscious, Daddy. When I looked up, it
was like ten guys in here. They tore my asshole up while I was out and
then raped me while I was conscious, too," she admitted with tears
forming in her eyes.

"Don't cry, baby," he comforted, while stroking her cheek. "What
was your take before this mayhem?"

"About fifteen hundred," Amber answered.

"That's a good night. Daddy is pleased, baby." King smiled, flashing
his diamond-encrusted gold upon his canine.

"Daddy, them niggas robbed me for the bread," she informed.

Right then, King's entire demeanor changed. Rena saw it as did the
rest of the girls. She jumped for joy within.

"So, you telling me you ain't got shit to show for the whole fucking
night?" he snapped.

"Daddy, it ain't her fault," Trina said.

Before she knew what had hit her, Trina was backslapped to the
floor.

"Bitch, you right! It's both of y'all hoes fault. It's your fault for bringing this stupid bitch to me and your fault for being a stupid ass bitch!" he barked.

Amber knew King wouldn't take to her losing the money but hoped for a little sympathy.

"I tell you hoes what. Y'all need to go get me my muthafucking money! You said you had fifteen hunnid for pimpin' and then ten more niggas sampled some of my merchandise? Oh, bitch, I need all that paper back up out that pussy tonight," he admonished.

"Tonight?" Amber questioned.

"Yes, bitch! Tonight, as in before the sunrise. I best have all mines, hoe! Ya dig?"

Amber took a little too long to answer his question. Rena knew that he loved when she took initiative. "Hello, you hear my daddy talking to you?" Rena spat, slapping Amber.

"Whoa, bitch. Not the face. She fucked up enough up that way. Teach her body a few things," King suggested.

The girls watched as Rena punched Amber in the belly and made her drop. Trina turned her head as Rena kicked and stomped on her friend. Any other time, she would have put her in her place, but King had silently sanctioned the abuse with his suggestion of approval.

Rena stood eye-to-eye with Amber, prepared to take out all of her insecurities on her. "You think some lame excuse is gonna get you off the hook with my daddy? You got life fucked up, bitch!"

Amber dropped to her knees once Rena threw a blow to her gut. The unsuspected attack took all of the wind out of Amber. Vomit spewed from her lips as she tried to regain her composure. King smirked as his girls went to work. Grabbing a hand full of hair, Rena yanked Amber's head back.

"Daddy don't want me to beat you in the face, but there's other ways to get my point across," she chastised.

Before Amber knew it, Rena was forcing her face down into her own vomit. King was disgusted yet very entertained. The other girls turned their heads away from the horrific sight. Amber was pissed, and that motivated her to fight back. She rose to her feet, turned to Rena, and charged at her. Taken aback, Rena found Amber mounting her.

"Hit her in the face and you'll have to deal with me next!" King reminded.

Taking his words into consideration, Amber held Rena by her wrists, pinning her down. Rena was defenseless. Amber reasoned how stupid the entire scenario was. Attempting to reason with her, she began to speak.

"Why are we doing this? I was gang-raped tonight and robbed. It could be you tomorrow. Instead of getting me help, I'm being forced to go through this unnecessary bullshit with you. This isn't right. Don't you see that?"

Rena saw her opportunity and seized it. "You're right. This whole thing is fucked all the way up."

As the pair whispered to one another, King grew curious. "What's all the chatter about, bitches?" he barked.

"Come on. Let's put an end to this shit," Rena suggested.

Relieved, Amber released her from her grip and attempted to help her up to her feet. Taking a hold of Amber's hand, Rena pulled herself up slightly before dropping all of her weight. Amber fell to the floor and the tables had turned. Punching Amber in the side, Rena jumped to her feet and began using them as weapons. The girls were mortified at the damage she was doing to Amber. Trina wanted to run over and help her friend so bad. She walked over to King and stood before him, venom filled her eyes.

"Hoe, what's on your mind?" he asked.

"I didn't bring her to you for you to treat her like this. For goodness sakes, the girl was just gang-raped, King," Trina reminded.

"And after this, she'll know not to let that shit happen again. Now, get out of my way before I forget who you are and carve your pretty lil face up," he threatened, revealing his switchblade.

Trina knew not to press him any further and stepped away. King smirked and continued to enjoy the spectacle. Rena blanked out as she kicked Amber in the ribs. She hated her sister with a passion and it showed.

Once King had had enough, he whistled for Rena to get back to his side. Amber fought back tears as she looked up from the floor to the women.

"Don't look at that bitch. She should feel the shame she's brought upon our family tonight. Turn y'all backs 'til she's redeemed herself," King commanded.

All of her so-called "sisters" turned away from facing Amber. Even Trina. King smirked as Amber climbed to her feet.

"Daddy, I'll make it up to you," she vowed, caressing his cheek.

"Bitch, don't touch me 'til you clean your hands with my cash. Now, go beat your feet, hoe. You on my time," he coldly replied.

Amber watched as they all left her alone in agonizing pain. Falling to the bed, she buried her face in her hands while the tears came pouring down. It wasn't long before she pulled herself together, took a hot shower, and left to hit the streets. She spent all night sucking and fucking from one end of town to the next in order to get King's coins.

As she hung on the corner, Amber looked at her watch. It was two in the morning. Her pussy was sore and asshole raw. She needed a new plan and fast! Spotting a few guys in a Waffle House, she figured she'd make her money back with one final stop. Entering the restaurant, she made her way over to the empty booth beside the fellas. All eyes were on her as she sat down. In no time, a waitress made her way over to take her order.

"Hold that thought. Hey, guys. What do you recommend I get to fill me up?" she asked with a provocative emphasis.

One turned and replied, "I like the steak and eggs myself."

Amber looked at the waitress. "Steak and eggs it is."

Once the waitress left, Amber focused on the table. "Now, which of you gentlemen are gonna pay for my steak and eggs?"

All the guys looked at the same guy who had spoken up before.

"I might as well. I'm taking care of all these ugly niggas's tabs over here. The least I could do is pay for a pretty woman's food," he smirked.

Amber saw where the money was. The other scrubs were useless and she now had her target. "How 'bout you come sit with this pretty lady then, sir?" she invited.

He quickly obliged her request.

"I'm Tasha," she lied.

"I'm Peter."

"Peter, I have a confession to make."

"What is it?" he wondered.

"I would much rather get filled up by you than those steak and eggs," she whispered.

Peter felt her foot caress his penis underneath the concealment of the table. He couldn't believe his stroke of fortune. "You're for real?"

"I ain't free. And I cost way more than that order. But yeah, I'm for real," she insisted.

"How much we talking?"

She smiled. "Three hundred to make all your nastiest dreams a reality."

Peter would've given her a grand to just taste it. He was loaded and lonely. "Cool! Where should we go?"

"I know a place."

After eating, Amber took him right back to her hotel and made him pay for another room. Watching all the bills he had in his wallet made her salivate. She had made up her mind that she was going to clip him for all of it. They headed upstairs where Amber stripped completely naked. Peter admired her flawless body as she stood in all of her splendor.

"Take your clothes off," she demanded.

Breaking out of his stupor, Peter began to get naked, as well. Once he was done, Amber pushed him on the bed and began to caress his balls. The feel of her tongue swiping across his earlobe sent chills through his entire frame. His dick began to rise to an impressive length as she began to slowly tug at it.

Peter squirmed as she licked from his ear down to his manhood. Placing her head in his lap, Amber swirled her tongue around his dick. The wetness and warmth of it nearly drove Peter insane. Reaching down, he clutched onto her shoulder as she took him down her throat. The gargling and gagging had Peter in a realm of ecstasy.

Amber had learned many tricks to her trade, and her aim was to fuck Peter to sleep. Savoring his centerpiece on her tonsils, she began to hum on it. The vibrations stirred something in Peter's soul. His climax began to shoot forth but wasn't quite ready to erupt. Fondling his balls, Amber reached up with her free hand to rub his chest.

Removing his penis briefly, she said, "Fuck me in my mouth!"

Peter placed both of his hands on the back of her head and began to pump viciously into her mouth. His forceful thrusts caused tears to run from her eyes, but she refused to run from the dick. Peter didn't take long before he began to cum without relent. The feel of her mouth sucking him down like a straw was too much to bear. He released her head and allowed her to take full control. Amber squeezed his nut into her mouth and swallowed down every single drop. Peter was in a state of euphoria as the last remnants of his seeds were slurped away.

Amber spun around and put her pussy in his mouth while she licked the sides of Peter's flaccid penis. She wanted to keep him aroused while she teased his dick back to full length. Peter grabbed a hold of Amber's juicy ass and gripped it tightly. Mashing his tongue against her clit, he lapped away at her honeycomb. Amber oozed into his mouth as he did a fine job feasting away.

Suddenly, his dick was back hard as a rock. Climbing away from his mouth, she mounted his member and slowly inched it inside of her warm body. Placing both of her hands in the middle of his chest, Amber used her Kegel skills to suck the life out of Peter's dick. He squeezed and pinched her nipples as she rode him like a cowgirl. Leaning forward, she began to suckle his neck and fuck him faster.

"Throw that dick in me, baby," she purred.

Peter felt like the man and did just that. Amber felt his manhood hitting her back walls as he began to go wild. She lost control as he rolled over on top and pinned her frame to the bed. Peter fucked her until she found herself cumming uncontrollably. Likewise, Peter followed suit and bust his second nut.

Collapsing onto her shoulder, he rolled over. "Let me get your money for you," he panted.

"No, baby. Let's rest a bit and wake up to some more of that," she insisted.

Peter felt like a king. He had a hoe wanting to get some more! Drifting off to sleep, Peter couldn't wait to awaken for another round. Yet, when he woke up, he only saw a lonely bed and empty wallet.

Amber was exhausted. She had finally returned with a bag, which pleased her daddy.

He smiled. "Now that's good hoeing," he complimented, welcoming her home.

Chapter 2

"Look at how good you've gotten at this, Amber," David acknowledged.

Amber couldn't help but blush as she pecked away at the computer keys. David was a blogger who worked for a local magazine company. He met Amber online and quickly requested her services. To her surprise, once he arrived at the motel, he broke out his cell phone and prepared to record her audio. Amber found that he wasn't interested in her body. He was interested in her mind.

David wanted to start a blog series about the life of a whore and the thought process behind her actions. At first, Amber saw her time with David as easy money. All she had to do was show up and get paid to talk about her day and how she felt about it. The problem was that the more she revealed, the more she thought, and that caused her to eventually evaluate her entire lifestyle. David picked up on her newfound reluctance to "the life" and began to encourage her to walk away from it.

With no real skills, Amber never fully entertained his ideas of a normal and decent life. David then came up with the strategy that he would help her learn how to type since nearly most jobs required such a skill. He even went to the extent of talking to his boss about hiring her for a spot at the magazine company.

"You sure you don't want to take this position at the company? It could be the break that you've been praying for," he said.

"How do you know what I pray for? Boy, you better stay out of me and God's business. Besides, it ain't that easy to just walk away. I mean, where would I live?" Amber reasoned.

"Live here! I mean, I got plenty of room until you can get on your feet," he offered.

Amber studied David. He was such a good guy. In the back of her mind, she wondered what it was that he saw in a hoe like her. He was truly a dream, but her reality was way too real for her to get caught up in a Prince Charming.

"David, I really appreciate all that you've done for me, but now just isn't the time. I'm not ready."

He reached down and took her tiny hands into his. "Well, if you ever change your mind, no matter the day or night, just call me. I will be there with nothing but opportunities for you."

Amber blushed and gave him a big hug. "It's time for me to get home."

"Come on. I'll give you a lift."

David knew the drill as he let her out down the street. King would beat the living shit out of her if she were to bring a trick to their front door. He waved goodbye and pulled off.

Amber smoothed out her mini skirt as she placed her key in the door of King's castle. Once she saw the bushes move on the side of the door, it was too late to react. A man sprouted from the greenery with two guns in her face. A second man appeared from the side of the house with an even larger gun strapped across his shoulder.

"Finish unlocking the door before I leave you stuck to it, bitch," one of the intruders ordered.

King sat sipping a glass of cognac as the door opened. His eyes grew huge once the trio entered.

"Nigga, where's my bread?" the man said, swinging the AK-47 on his shoulder into his hands and aiming at King and his girls.

All of the women clung to one another in fear. Trina froze in place away from the crowd. Amber trembled as the other man holding two guns placed them on each side of her head. She collapsed to her knees in fear and tears.

"Pl—please d—don't kill—kill me," she begged.

"Bitch ass nigga! You hear me talking to you?"

King jumped to his feet. "I got your money, man. Come on, Melo. You ain't got to do all this."

"Get me my money before I have this hoe brains all over your cheap ass carpet," Melo ordered.

King sent Rena to go and grab a specific duffle bag. Once she returned with it, Melo made her count every single bill in front of everyone. The tension in the room was so thick, you could cut it with a knife. Rena silently prayed that it was all there. When she was finished, Melo was pleased to see that it was all there.

"See, man. I told you I was going to square everything with you," King said.

"Bring me my money," Melo replied.

Rena moved to follow his instructions, but Melo pointed his weapon, causing her to stop dead in her tracks.

"Not you . . . him."

King slowly did as he was told. He grabbed the bag and as soon as he got within reaching distance, Melo took the butt of his weapon and slammed it into King's head. Once he hit the floor, Melo stomped him relentlessly as the girls begged for him to stop. Amber took the moment she had to crawl away from her captor.

Once Melo was done, he spit on King. "Stick to pimpin', you bitch ass nigga. You damn sure ain't no drug dealer. I would kill you, but I know how much you love your hoes. Kebo!" Melo exclaimed.

At the sound of his name, he knew what to do. Scanning the room, he found the lone sheep. With six shots, Kebo killed Trina in cold blood. Her body fell directly in front of Amber. The latter was paralyzed. She wanted to scream, but no sound came out. Everything began to move in slow motion as Trina stared lifelessly back at Amber. The tears poured heavily as everyone gathered around their dead "sister".

****

It had been weeks since Trina's shotgun funeral and business as usual for everyone except Amber. She had awakened to David's words and found herself needing a way out. The two had talked about her leaving

King more often, and David could see he was finally getting through to her. All she needed was his courage to break ties, and he was ready to lend it.

Pulling up in front of King's home, David parked and prepared to exit the vehicle.

"No, I got to do this on my own. If I ain't out in five minutes, then bust in that muthafucka like my life depends on it, 'cause it probably will," she teased.

David watched as she retrieved her suitcase and headed out. Checking his semi-automatic, he was ready for whatever was to come.

Rena was the first to spot Amber storm into the house. She could tell by her demeanor and the big ass suitcase in her hand that she was up to something. Without hesitation, she dashed off to go and alert King.

Amber moved at lightning speed as she stuffed her clothes into the luggage. Once she had everything she needed, Amber raced back downstairs to find King waiting for her.

With his arms folded across his chest, he smiled. "Going somewhere, baby?"

"I'm done, King. This life isn't the life for me anymore," Amber said, attempting to walk by.

King remained calm as Rena stood directly in front of Amber, trying to block her smooth getaway. The rest of the girls sat back idle, waiting to see how King would handle a renegade.

"What makes you think you can just walk out on me? Hoe, I chose you! You ain't done 'til I say you done and there ain't no way out of this shit unless I put you in the casket. You pick a casket out yet, bitch?" King taunted, releasing his switchblade.

The sight of the sharp object compelled Amber to quake. "King, I'm walking out of that door. You can't stop me. Hell, you can't even protect us!" she exclaimed, finding her strength.

King grew furious.

"Bitch, you getting out of line!" Rena spat, charging at Amber.

Ready for combat, Amber slipped her hand into her pocket. She had stashed a pair of brass knuckles in there. Getting her tiny fingers into them, she hurriedly dropped her bag and threw up her guard. Rena was too busy trying to impress King to notice the heavy-duty jewelry on her fist. The second Rena lightened up, Amber broke her nose with one blow. Blood trickled down her face as she crumbled up like a piece of balled up paper.

With vicious kicks to her stomach, Amber preached. "Look-at-you-now-bitch! This-nigga-can't-save-you-like-he-ain't-save-Trina!"

The rest of the women looked on in awe.

King had enough. "Ungrateful bitch! Say hey to Trina when you see her," he said, leaping towards his prey.

Amber grabbed her suitcase from the floor and ran for the door. She yanked open the door to reveal David aiming his gun. King froze in place.

"I was just about to kick this door down. You good?" David asked with his weapon focused on King.

"Yeah, I was just saying my good byes," Amber replied, catching her breath.

David looked beyond King at the obvious fright on the girls' faces. Then he saw Rena moaning in pain. He smiled while escorting her out. King watched helplessly as another man walked away with his top-earning hoe.

Slamming the door, he turned to the rest of his stable, prepared to scare the bravery out of the rest of them. "First of all, before you hoes go thinking you can just walk out on me, know that you got another thing coming. Ain't nobody safe who choose to walk out that door. After I've taken you in, clothed you, fed you, managed you, and spent my precious time on you, you think your ungracious ass just going to walk out on me? Nah, you bitches make it your business to keep tabs on her and learn everything about that nigga she with. Ol' punk ass, square muthafucka thinks it's sweet. It ain't over 'til I say it's over and you can mark my words that this shit has just begun!"

Chapter 3

Things appeared to be going smoothly for Amber. She took David's advice and moved in with him until she could get on her own feet. He was pleased that she finally took the position at his magazine company and began earning income by legal means.

Amber broke down in tears after receiving her first real paycheck. David was right by her side to comfort her as the two finally made love. He looked into Amber's eyes and the feelings they both felt were undeniable.

She got on her tippy toes and placed her lips against his. David pulled her body closer to his while grasping her by the waist. As his tongue explored the inner confines of her mouth, Amber began to unbutton his shirt. Next, she moved down to his pants. Unzipping his fly, she felt his manhood protruding through the fabric of his boxers. As she began to lower herself, Amber felt his arms grip her shoulders. Confused, she looked up at him.

He raised her back tall. "Its your turn to be catered to."

Amber gave away her control and allowed him to move her over to his bed. Placing her upon its edge, he slid his hand up her dress and pulled her panties off. Lying back on her elbows, Amber anticipated what was next to come. Her heart was beating a million miles per hour.

David hiked her dress up and bowed in between her thighs, observing her stiffened clit. Amber moved her crumpled up dress out of the way so she could look down and see him. David took one of her legs and lifted it above his shoulder. Resting her calf muscle on his shoulder, he spread her other leg a bit further apart.

Next, he stuck his tongue out and placed the tip of it along the bottom of her clit. Pressing it against her tender flesh, he swirled his tongue counterclockwise around her clit. The feeling he created was electric. Adding his full lips to the equation, David began to suck her clit into his mouth like a hungry baby did its bottle.

Amber reached down to clutch his shoulders as she came in his mouth. The feeling of her body trembling only encouraged David to give her more oral ecstasy. Amber found herself enjoying two more orgasms before David removed his boxers and unleashed his manhood. It was perfect. Not too long or thick but just perfect! She began salivating at the sight of it.

Climbing onto the bed, David positioned himself on the side of her. It was as if he was silently stating that they were equals. Neither beneath or above the other, but side by side, no matter how the world chose to view either of the two. A tear slowly crept down her cheek from the thrustful force he gave. Penetrating much more than her core, David had managed to penetrate her heart, as well.

Throwing her leg over his, Amber wanted him closer. She dug her nails into his chest as with each gentle stroke after stroke, she felt his length fill her up to capacity. Placing her tongue in his mouth, she relished the traces of her cum that still remained.

With eager satisfaction, David plowed away at her womb as he gripped her ass cheeks. He was always attracted to her. What man in his right mind wouldn't be? It was just the life that she chose to lead made her an enigma. He saw so much promise in Amber's future, but she would have to see it for herself.

Lying on his back, he afforded her the opportunity to ride him and she did. Lifting him up eye level, she leaned back in his lap with her arms around his neck. As she grinded on his manhood, she never broke eye contact and neither did he. David hit spots that Amber forgot she had. Those spots that she had to numb in order to live "the life".

King took a vulnerable girl and used her to his advantage, but here was David. A man who took her as the woman she was and went out of his way to treat her with the respect that she deserved. For the first time in her life, copulation wasn't her occupation. It was a mutual connection and, in that moment, she felt a love that she wanted to feel forever.

As David reached his climax, simultaneously, Amber reached hers. The pair came in one another's arms and knew from that point on, things would never be the same. Everything seemed to be falling in place for Amber. She was beginning to see that her life in "the life" was merely an illusion. King was the master illusionist of a world producing nothing but self-destruction.

After a long day at work, Amber was elated to finally be getting off. She couldn't wait to get home and into her man's loving arms. Likewise, David anticipated her arrival.

He heard the front door open and made his way into the living room. "Babe, you're home early." Holding a cup of warm coffee in hand, he froze as his eyes looked up into King's menacing stare.

"Didn't know you were expecting me?" King teased with his gun in hand.

David quickly tossed his coffee into King's face. The hot substance stung as soon as it landed on his skin. David used King's temporary moment of weakness to further attack. Charging him to the ground, he fought to remove the weapon from his hand.

King took David's vicious blows as best he could while trying to regain his vision. He was losing the grip on his pistol, so he had to drop it in order to fight David off. Mounting on top of his opponent, David laid stiff punches into King's jaw. Attempting to shift his body weight, King squirmed underneath his frame.

Suddenly, he caught his first break. David released him in a move to get to the gun. King lunged his knee into his nuts and chomped down on his ear like a mad man. David felt the pain of King's teeth tearing through his flesh as he jerked away. Crawling back against the wall, David reached his hand up to his ear and felt dangling meat. Blood poured from the side of his head as he watched King chew and spit out a large piece of his ear. Rising to his feet, King picked up his gun and watched as David raced into his bedroom and slammed the door behind him.

"I'll huff and I'll puff and I'll be forced to blow your door down if you don't open up, Lil Davie," King taunted with a hearty laugh.

After a few seconds, he had had enough. King raised his foot and kicked the door in. To his surprise, David was there waiting with an aluminum baseball bat. Before King could react, David smacked him across the head with it. Again, the gun flew from his grip. King fell against the wall and shook off the vicious blow.

"Come on, you punk piece of shit," David urged.

King smirked and looked down at his gun. He knew he wouldn't get to it before David knocked his head off, so he chose to improvise.

"I tell you what, Davie boy. Put that bat down and I won't have Amber cut into a million pieces," he said. David was confused. "That's right, give her a call and see that she won't answer. My girls got her. If you want her back, then you need to drop that bat and let me walk away."

David wasn't trying to hear it, but he couldn't chance it. Turning towards his phone gave King the split second that he needed to act. Racing towards him, King tackled him onto the bed. He placed David in a chokehold, rolled over onto his back, and squeezed away for dear life. David fought to break free as he looked towards the ceiling, but it was to no avail. The bat slowly fell from his hand as tears streamed down his cheeks. Gagging for breath, David fell unconscious.

King smiled as he felt David's body go limp. Pushing David off of him, he stood tall, smoothed his clothes out, preparing himself to find some duct tape or rope. As King found what he was looking for, he felt overjoyed at how Amber would look once she got home. He couldn't believe she had the audacity to try to outsmart him and go her separate ways. In his mind, she was trying to prove to the rest of his stable that they didn't need him, as well.

He could not let that go on unanswered. Either they would feel he couldn't manage them and move on to another pimp or see Amber's independence as a motivator to pursue their own. No way! A whore was nothing more than a whore, and today, Amber was about to be reminded of that big fact.

King dragged David's body and sat him in a chair. Then he stuffed his mouth with a sock he'd pulled from his own foot. Binding his wrists and feet, King admired his work.

"Yeessss, you cool ass muthafucka, you!" He giggled. "My man, you got some pimpin' in ya' blood, but you just knocked the wrong nigga, hoe." King smiled, backing away to wait on the lady of the evening to return.

****

Happy that David had given her so much, Amber couldn't wait to get home and place kisses on his lips. She was so caught up in euphoria, that she never noticed Rena tailing her car.

"She's pulling into the driveway, Daddy," Rena said into her cell.

"Thanks, baby. Time to show this hoe who's the boss," King replied, clicking off.

He looked over at David. He had him tied to a chair in his own bedroom. King stood with his pistol in hand. "My hoe is home. She'll be joining us in just a sec, so sit tight," he joked.

David was gagged and couldn't produce anything but mumbled words as he sat strapped down. Amber retrieved her house keys as Rena made her way over to her. Amber couldn't believe her eyes when she looked up.

"Hey, sis." Rena waved with King's switchblade in hand.

As she rushed to get inside, Amber unlocked her door only to find King with a gun to David's head. She was paralyzed with fear. Rena pushed her inside and quickly closed the door behind them.

"So you thought you were just going to abandon ship and leave me hanging, huh?" King questioned.

"Please, let him go. This is between us, not him. He isn't a part of our world," Amber pleaded.

King smiled. "You sure? This nigga got to have some pimpin' in his blood to come and snatch one of my hoes. Hell, my top dollar bitch at that!"

"Give me the word, Daddy. I'll trash this traitor right here," Rena spoke, anxious to end her once and for all.

"Hold tight, baby doll. I want to see how much Macaroni Tony mean to this bitch. So now, give me a reason to keep this nigga breathing."

Amber's eyes began to twinkle with a glimpse of hope. "I will leave with you! I will come back and never leave your side. I'll be your best earner and never complain. Please, just spare him!"

Rena didn't like the sounds that were coming out of her mouth. Even more so, she detested the way it seemed King was receptive to what she was said.

"You can't trust this conniving muthafucka," Rena said, grabbing Amber by her ponytail.

King watched as she snatched her head back and placed the blade upon it. "Nah, I think you're wrong, Rena. I believe this bitch has seen the light. Let her go," he ordered.

Reluctant, Rena released her grip. Amber looked forward at David.

"I believe you, baby, but I need some insurance that you won't ever be persuaded again," King said before squeezing the trigger.

Amber jumped as she watched a bullet enter into David's head and exit out the other side.

"No!" she cried out.

King laughed. Rena followed his lead.

Amber's pain transformed into hatred as she grabbed a hold of Rena. "I'm going to kill you!" Amber promised, strangling the girl.

Defending herself, Rena sliced Amber from her forehead, all the way down to her chin. Blood began to pour and Amber stumbled backwards.

"Shit!" King exclaimed, not wanting his product's value depreciated. Dropping his pistol into David's lap, King leaped in front of Amber in order to grab onto Rena's swinging wrist. "Calm the fuck down! This bitch still got to make money for me and you fucking her up. Cool out!"

"Baby, watch out!" Rena exclaimed.

King turned around to find Amber aiming his pistol directly at him. His instincts kicked in, as he pulled Rena in front of him. Using her as a shield, he backed out of the house as Rena's torso took bullet after bullet.

Amber blacked out as blood filled her eyes. King dropped Rena's lifeless corpse in the doorway and fled the scene as fast as he could. Amber ran outside the house screaming at the top of her lungs. Placing the gun to her head, she squeezed the trigger. Fortunately, the clip was empty.

She collapsed in the middle of the street, crying and punching the pavement until her knuckles were broken. Neighbors alerted the authorities to the scene. Finding her frantic with two dead bodies nearby, they attempted to cart Amber off to jail, but she wasn't having it. Hysterical, she figured she had nothing at all left to lose and everything to gain.

Racing to her car, the cops watched in disbelief as she went after King. As she sped away from the scene, officers hopped in their vehicles and prepared to give chase as well as call for more back up. Amber was focused as she wiped tears from her eyes and flushed through traffic until she spotted King.

Looking in his rearview, King couldn't believe his eyes. Amber drove like a bat out of hell as she smashed into the back of his vehicle. The impact nearly broke his neck. Gaining composure, he looked back to see that she had hurt herself, as well. Amber's head smacked against the steering wheel upon the collision. Shaking off her dizziness, she looked up to find King speeding away. His actions prompted her to smash the gas, as well.

Cop cars, with their sirens blaring, flew in pursuit of her. King looked at the stream of officers tailing her as he darted through traffic. He was relieved to see them. Amber caught up to his car and began to pull up alongside him. He looked out his passenger window and saw her crash into his side.

As he swerved, King nearly missed an oncoming semi truck. "Fucking bitch!" he exclaimed.

"I'm gonna kill you!" she retorted.

Again, she smashed into his side, causing him to crash into another vehicle. This time, his body flew through the windshield and landed onto the street. Cars swerved and crashed into one another in order to avoid hitting the bloody lump of flesh lying in the street. King was barely breathing but held on as he turned to lay on his back. Hearing Amber's voice gave him the strength to raise up.

"Die, muthafucka!" she screamed, placing the medal to the floor.

King looked on as her car sped at him. There was nothing he could do. He simply embraced his demise with a smile as she darted for him. Suddenly, the sun shined down on a pimp. A police car fishtailed Amber from behind, causing her to spin out into a nearby car. The impact knocked her out instantly. Piling out of their cars, the officers surrounded her vehicle with their weapons drawn. King couldn't believe his good fortune as they rushed him into the medics.

****

Dr. Sheldon studied Amber as she sat in front of him in visitation. He had been assigned to study her behavioral advances to see if she was mentally competent to stand trial. Nearly a month had gone by since her arrest and no progress had been made. Yet, the doctor hoped that today would be different. Today, Amber would be receiving her first visitor.

Rising from his seat, the doctor went to open the door. Amber came alive once King entered the room.

"I'll let you two talk in private," Dr. Sheldon said, exiting.

King simply nodded and then smiled at Amber. "Look at you. Look at what that simp made of you," he said and smirked.

With her hands cuffed to the table before her, Amber was again helpless. "Fuck you! You piece of shit! One day, you'll get what you deserve!" she spat with nothing more than her words to defend herself.

King folded his arms across his chest and laughed. "Oh, you're mad at me for what? Baby, I taught you the rules to this shit long ago. You chose to break them and now here are the consequences. Dead niggas, lengthy sentences, and crazy bitches! All 'cause you wanted to be more than a WHORE," he said and snickered.

In her mind, King was right. David would still be alive had she stuck to the game. Wanting out "the life", ultimately ruined her life. The reality of it all drove Amber insane. Dr. Sheldon raced into the room with officers as she began to scream and become belligerent.

Ushering King out, the officers then subdued the young woman by force. Her mental state was clear to Dr. Sheldon at that point. Preparing his evaluation case for the courts, he turned in his findings on young Amber. After a period, she was deemed unfit for trial and sentenced to an insane asylum for the mentally incompetent. Scarred for life, she was forced to reside with the company of crazies for the rest of her days.

As for King, he continued pimpin' and found a new state to settle his hoes in. Without missing a beat, he maintained his motto, which was *there was no business like his hoe business*. In a just world, King would've ended up incarcerated for the lives he destroyed. Furthermore, Amber could've lived happily ever after with her knight in shining armor, David. Yet, it isn't a just world in the streets. It's just the world Amber lived in as a WHORE.

The End

URBAN AESOP

BLEED LIKE ME

POLICE LINE —

HOOD CHRONICLES

BLEED LIKE ME
A Short Story by
Hood Chronicles

Prologue

Lil James took a look at the gun his friend had just placed in his hand. The teen had seen plenty of artillery in the streets of Atlanta, but the forty-five he was now holding had a special purpose. Derek, his best friend, had arrived with Antonio on a mission. The three young men were tired of being broke and had half-heartedly come to the conclusion that they were going to hit a lick for some fast cash.

"Listen," Derek began. "Ain't no need in punking out at the last minute. Y'all niggas still down right?"

"Yea!" the other two said in unison.

"Cool, cause I'm ready to get this bread," he said and chuckled. All of the boys shared in laughter when the door suddenly pushed open. They all froze as Lil James tried to hide the gun behind his back. The boys looked up to see Lil James's big brother step inside.

"What's up, Hood?" they greeted.

"What's the word?" Hood replied, embracing the fellas. Once he got to his brother, Hood could sense that something was off.

"What's that you got behind your back?" he questioned. Lil James, as well as his friends, began to grow nervous. Hood Chronicles was one of the coolest old heads that they knew, but they each also knew that he wasn't for the bullshit.

"I'm waiting," Hood said, growing impatient. A bit afraid, Lil James revealed the forty-five to his brother. Hood quickly turned and shut the door to his little brother's bedroom. "What in the hell do you have that for?" Hood inquired.

"It's mine," Derek spoke up.

"Okay, lil nigga. What do you got that for?" Derek began to look at the floor. "Nah, look at me like a man! If you're grown enough to tote a tool around that can end someone's entire existence, then you got to be grown enough to look me in my eyes and explain this shit," Hood snapped.

Derek lifted his head and stared Hood directly in his eyes. "You've been out here in these streets. You know how this shit goes, Hood. We out here trying to get to the money and this piece right here is going to secure our bag." Hood smirked, then looked to his brother and Antonio.

"That's how y'all feel? A gun going to get y'all riches, huh? Lil nigga, a gun got me a whole lot of time in the penitentiary regretting that I ever picked that bitch up. So what y'all supposed to be a robbing crew, now?"

"We ain't saying all of that. We just going to hit this one lick for some bread," Antonio replied. Hood began to laugh at the young boys naive nature.

"Let me tell y'all something. If this shit y'all got planned go wrong, then you might be looking at some real hard time, or else the grave. I know that y'all ain't ready for neither one of those options. But, if you get away with this, it'll be worse. It's like drugs. After that first hit of the street life, you'll be hooked. Lick after lick increases risk after risk," Hood enlightened.

Derek let out a huge sigh of grief, not really caring to hear a lecture. Hood shook his head knowing that too many young black males didn't listen until it was usually too late.

"Okay, I can see that you're not really interested in what I'm saying, so how about I tell you like this? You can get killed or kill somebody going out there with that. A life sentence is a mandatory thirty years before you're even looked at by the parole board. Shit gets real!" Hood explained.

"That's a long time," Lil James gasped.

"Man, we ain't getting no life sentences!" Derek assured.

"What if we get shot, though?" Antonio questioned.

"We ain't getting shot neither!"

Hood folded his arms across his chest. "You sure got it all figured out," he said. Derek's head was spinning. Deep down inside, he was afraid and needed to feed off of his friend's courage. Hood could see right through him. Hood took the gun and made the boys sit down on the bed.

"Tell y'all what. Nobody was there to make me sit my ass down and take heed so I'm not going to force y'all either. I just want to share a little story with you young kings. After that, the choice is yours. Fair?" All three teens looked at each other and then shook their heads in agreement. "Alright, well here's a little tale that I like to call Bleed Like Me..."

Chapter 1

Cyrus looked down in his lap at his Glock 40. It was his favorite se-mi-automatic weapon. It's chrome caused the sunlight to dance off of it with a glare of refined splendor whenever he flexed on niggas in the daytime. Yet, at this very moment, it was pitch black in the heart of the night. Holding his Glock up, he placed an extended clip inside of his baby. Looking over his shoulder, Cyrus began to speak to his partners in crime.

"Y'all niggas ready back there?" he questioned to the two men seated in the back of the Chevy Caprice.

"Nigga, I stay ready," Theo replied, holding up a double barrel shotgun. He was the largest of the group. With muscles stacked on top of muscles, Theo struck fear into the average man, woman, and child by just being present. At 6'6", he was tall, dark, and hideous. Yea, Theo had the face that only a mother could love. Since his mother had passed when he was a child, he settled for the love of his thug brother, Jewels.

Jewels looked to the front seat at Cyrus and said, "I'm trying to get to this money. Nigga, is you finished or is you done talking?"

Theo and Cyrus shared a chuckle. Jewels was the humble, yet most deadly of the clique. He got the nickname Jewels from his success as an armed robber. He would single-handedly run up on the most danger-ous dope boys and make them hand over their money and jewels. He was cool as a cucumber, but a special kind of crazy when provoked.

Gripping his 50 caliber Desert Eagle, Jewels opened his door and prepared to exit the vehicle. Theo followed suit. Cyrus looked over at Johnny. He peeped how sweaty the young boys palms were. Johnny wasn't a part of the clique. He was only sixteen and wanted so bad to get money with the infamous trio known as the Bad News Bandits. Fig-uring the kid could come in handy as a getaway driver, Cyrus enlisted the youngin'.

"Don't fuck this opportunity up, little nigga. When I get out, pull the car up the street by the streetlight. We going to be coming out through the woods. Be fucking ready!" Cyrus ordered.

"I got you, big homie," Johnny assured. Cyrus could tell that he was nervous. He knew that he had good reason to be as he flashed a friendly smile. Hopping out, Cyrus pulled his ski mask over his face and quickly joined Theo and Jewels as they crept through the night. Jewels led the trio because he was the one who set the entire mission up.

A few months prior, he met Cindy at the club, easily making her fall in love. Well, Cindy was Brick's lady and Brick got his name from being the kilo weight man in the city. After coercing Cindy into helping him set Brick up, Jewels needed his bandits to help bring the bad news to Brick's doorstep. Creeping silently around back, the trio awaited for their signal to move. In a matter of minutes, the gang saw the lights in the back room go out, then come back on. Next, the back door cracked open.

"That's our cue!" Jewels exclaimed as he raised up to the door. Following suit, the guys marched in behind him with their weapons drawn. Cindy stood with her back to the kitchen just like her and Jewels had discussed. Brick sat in the living room with two of his henchmen. They were busy at work. One of the goons was preoccupied, running bills through the money machine, while the other was stuffing kilo after kilo into multiple duffle bags.

"Jackpot, muthafuckas!" Jewels cried out, snatching Cindy into his arms and placing his pistol to her head. Theo quickly aimed his shotgun at the money counter before he could foolishly attempt to grab his weapon.

"That wouldn't be smart," Cyrus teased with his Glock pointed at the man filling the bags with coke. Brick sat in between the two men with nothing on his mind but the welfare of his beloved lady.

"Take it all, man. Just let my baby go," he pleaded. Jewels began to chuckle. Cyrus was amazed at how easy the lick had been going. He wanted to pat Jewels on the back.

"Finish filling a bag with coke! And you, fill one of them duffels with all that cash," Cyrus directed. Brick eagerly helped his men do as they were instructed. Jewels was pleased as he gripped Cindy's ass in front of Brick. "I see why you wouldn't want a hair harmed on this soft piece of tail," he joked. Brick was furious but fought to maintain his composure. Cyrus drugged the six bags to where Jewels stood and realized that they had a small problem.

"We never anticipated having to carry this much shit back out there through the woods. We're going to have to take multiple trips," he reasoned. Jewels figured that that would only slow them down, increasing the odds of the men doing something stupid. Within seconds, he had come up with an all-new game plan that didn't involve any risk factors.

"Where's your keys to that pretty ass truck out there in the back?" Jewels questioned. Brick hurriedly retrieved them from his pockets and tossed them to Cyrus. "Load that shit up and we going to be out," Jewels ordered.

Theo stayed planted firmly with his shotgun ready to blow. Cyrus quickly loaded up the truck and was ready to bounce.

"Alright, everything is secure. Let's ride out," he smiled. Brick became relieved. Jewels released Cindy and pushed her into her man's arms. As he squeezed her tight with love, Jewels laughed.

"Stupid ass niggas! Still loving these nothing ass hoes," he said. Cindy looked at Jewels in disbelief as he continued.

"That bitch is the reason I knew how to get to you. I knew when you would be getting your supply ready, counting money, and even when to come in. How you think all of that was possible?" Brick paused and looked Cindy's eyes. He could read the betrayal in them as pain coursed through his veins.

"No, how could you?" Brick asked as tears began to swell in his eyes.

"Cause I been dicking that bitch down for months!" Jewels exclaimed. Howling in frustration, Brick went for his pistol and caught three hollow tips in his face from Jewels's weapon. Cindy began to scream as fragments of his flesh and blood splattered all over her.

"What the fuck are you doing? Let's roll!" Cyrus snapped.

"Bitch, shut it up! I liked you better with my dick in your mouth," Jewels retorted, sending a single bullet into her forehead. At that point, Brick's goons realized that their only options were to die or run. Theo didn't hesitate to slaughter the men with his shotgun. Blood painted the walls of the living room and Cyrus was stuck in disbelief.

"Have you lost your damn mind? None of this had to take place!" Cyrus spat.

"We got to get out of here. I'm sure the neighbors heard the shots," Theo spoke.

"I'm sure the whole fucking block heard the shots!" Cyrus exclaimed.

Jewels remained his nonchalant self. "Bring the car around and me and Theo will meet you out front," he said.

"What?" Cyrus questioned.

"There's a safe upstairs. Nigga, we need that."

Cyrus looked at Jewels like he was crazy before responding. "We have more than enough. Let's just get the hell out of here."

"Just go! We will meet you out front," Jewels demanded. Cyrus looked at Theo.

"We'll be right out," the huge man assured. Against his better judgment, Cyrus did as he was told. Once he was gone, he pointed for Theo to head up the staircase. Concealing his weapon, Jewels reached down and retrieved Brick's gun from the floor. Theo looked around the bedroom and tore it apart. Heading into the walk-in closet, he searched it but came up with nothing.

"Jewels! I don't see no safe in here anywhere."

"I know. Goodbye, old friend," Jewels silently spoke. Theo turned to face his one time brother. Jewels raised Brick's gun and shot Theo in his neck. Collapsing to his knees, Theo looked into Jewels's heartless stare before everything went black. Next, Cyrus sat out front awaiting his accomplices.

"What the fuck is taking them so long?" he questioned to no one in particular. At that moment, Cyrus spotted the front door fly open. He couldn't believe his eyes. Jewels was flagging him down, telling him to come back to the house. Anxious for the night to be over, he raced at top speed to see what was so urgent.

"What's going on?" Cyrus inquired.

"There was somebody hiding upstairs. They shot Theo. I need you to help me carry him to the truck," Jewels informed.

"Shit! Was he hit up bad?" Cyrus asked, running upstairs.

"Nah, he going to make it," Jewels lied with a smirk.

Heading into the bedroom, Cyrus looked around. "Where is he?"

Without hesitation, Jewels came in opening fire. A hot bullet tore through Cyrus's arm, causing him to react swiftly. Unleashing his weapon, the wounded man dove into the closet. Viewing his friend's body lying lifeless on the floor, Cyrus turned towards the entrance and fired back. Jewels covered himself by diving behind the bed. Unaware of where Jewels had disappeared to, Cyrus rose to his feet and pinned his back against the wall. Looking from right to left, he could hear the police sirens in the wind drawing near.

"Fuck!" Cyrus exclaimed in an attempt to flee. Right then, Jewels popped up and let off three shots into his partner in crime's back. Cyrus dropped his pistol and fell to the floor. Blood gushed from his open wounds as his vision began to blur. "Why?" he faintly moaned as Jewels kneeled down and placed his gun to his head.

"It ain't no reason. I just want it all and don't like sharing," Jewels replied. Cyrus reached up with a burst of energy and clawed Jewels in his eyes.

"Aaahhhh shit!" he cried out in pain.

Cyrus pulled himself up to his feet and tried to escape but to no avail. As soon as he made it to the staircase, Jewels emptied the clip. Bullets ripped through his chest and legs. Cascading down a flight of stairs, Cyrus felt his jaw break once he reached the bottom. Hearing the sirens growing louder and louder, Jewels hopped over Cyrus's body and raced outside to the truck.

In no time, he was cruising away from the scene while a police car was arriving. Upon leaving the house, Jewels swerved off the road and instead of walking through the woods, he drove as far as he could through it. Once he could see Johnny parked at a safe distance from the trail, he abandoned the truck to retrieve Johnny. The pair made several trips back and forth to transport the bags from the truck to the trunk of the car.

Meanwhile, officers raced out with their weapons drawn. With the front door open, it was plain to see multiple homicides. The senior officer directed his men inside to the gory sight of bodies stretched out everywhere. Searching the house, the police all met back up in the living room to convene. Brick was a well-known drug dealer, so the cops had already figured the incident was drug related.

"Look," one of the officers said, pointing at Cyrus. He was struggling to breathe with his senses shot. Checking his pulse, the senior officer was relieved to have one potential witness or suspect, still alive for the moment. It wasn't long before the ambulance had arrived and loaded Cyrus inside to cart him off. Watching the police cars and EMTs fly by, Jewels placed the last duffle bag into the trunk of the Caprice. Johnny was beyond spooked and it showed.

"Where is everybody else, Jewels? This just doesn't feel right at all."

"Johnny, the guys are alright. Quit fucking worrying so much. Give me the keys so we can go pick them up on the other side of the woods." Johnny handed over the keys to Jewels.

"Wait a minute. We forgot a bag in the truck. Hurry up and let's go get it," Jewels said. Making their way back into the woods, Johnny never saw it coming.

"This is where we part ways, kid," were the final words the boy heard before Jewels gunned him down in cold blood.

Chapter 2

Fifteen years had slowly drifted by for Cyrus inside of the Georgia Penitentiary system. After his life was spared by the Almighty's mercy, he was charged with the gruesome murders of everyone in Brick's home that night. The courts showed no leniency on sentencing him to five consecutive life sentences. It would have been six, but the case surrounding Johnny's dead body couldn't be linked back to Cyrus. He knew that with all of his appeal motions exhausted, he was destined to die behind the wall.

On the flip side, Jewels had gotten off scot-free and made a name for himself in the game. He had taken all of his cash from the robbery and invested in an exotic car rental company. Jewels also took the free kilos of cocaine and increased his finances. Highly respected in the trenches, as well as Corporate America, he truly had the best of both worlds.

From time to time, Cyrus would get a glimpse of his old friend on the television screen. It ate him up inside to witness the snake living so high while he himself had been reduced to the lowest of the low. Cyrus had been placed on the mental health caseload because of several failed suicide attempts. He now utilized medication to quiet the thoughts of self-mutilation and ultimate annihilation.

The only friend he had was a homosexual by the name of Sugar who was getting out soon. Cyrus wasn't gay, but liked Sugar because he was loyal and harder than a lot of the so-called thugs he had met in his lifetime. Sugar wasn't attracted to Cyrus, but liked him because he never judged him for who he was.

Truth is, if you weren't around Sugar, you never know he was gay. He wasn't the flaming flamboyant type. He was reserved and only fucked with the guys who perpetrated the straight lifestyle, but we're living alternative as hell on the low. He would then put them on blast and beat the shit out of them when they jumped bad.

Truth be told, it was Sugar that talked Cyrus out of all of his self-destructiveness. The two began getting money together and formed a bond. They had the perfect scheme. All of the females liked to talk girl talk with Sugar so he got close to them. The corrections officers became his mules hauling in all types of drugs. Sugar wanted to keep a low profile, so he utilized Cyrus as the go-to guy. If anybody got wrong, Sugar didn't hesitate to slice off their body parts for payment. The day had come when it was time to say farewell. Sugar walked with Cyrus as far as the officers would permit before having to part ways.

"Listen, I told you that I am still here for you. No matter what you need, just call," Sugar said.

"Thanks. If I ever need to take you up on that offer, then believe I will. For now, just take care of yourself," Cyrus replied.

Sugar embraced his friend and waved goodbye as he exited through the back gate. It was a bittersweet moment for Cyrus. He was happy to see his friend free, but hated to see him go. Heading back to the dormitory, Cyrus walked into a situation that would mean more to him than he could possibly have known at that very moment.

A newbie had come through the doors and was considered fresh meat. Cyrus spotted a few inmates surrounding the kid. He knew their style and that given the opportunity, they would make him their bitch for the duration of his time confined. Cyrus figured that the he couldn't be any more than eighteen. Shrugging his shoulders, Cyrus figured it was none of his business and began to walk away. That's when the frightened boy said something that caused him to stop in his tracks.

"Please don't hurt me. My family has money and I can pay you guys for protection. My big brother is Jewels Streeter!"

Cyrus couldn't believe his ears. He turned back around and stared at the kid. The more he looked at him, he could see all of Jewels features in the boy. Cyrus could even recall holding the kid in his arms as a baby. He raced over to the head of the crew and unleashed his shank. The leader never saw it coming. Cyrus grabbed him by the collar of his shirt and placed his weapon to his neck. Everyone froze. They knew that a nigga who had tried to kill himself on several occasions didn't give a fuck about killing the next man.

"Nobody, and I mean nobody touches this kid!" he barked.

"Alright!" the man exclaimed in an attempt to keep himself from crossing over to the other side.

Cyrus released him and showed the kid to his cell. Thoroughly grateful, Jewels's little brother introduced himself as Rodney. Cyrus could tell that the kid was nothing like his brother. Jewels's money afforded him a lifestyle of privilege. A lifestyle that produced naivety. It didn't take long for Cyrus to befriend Rodney and find out all that he needed to know about the movements of Jewels. Cyrus had waited an entire year to put his plan into motion. He laid back on his bunk with a huge smile on his face. Rodney was currently in visitation with his big brother and once it was over, Cyrus would finally have his pay back.

****

Kicked back with his feet stretched out, Jewels sipped a glass of cognac as his chauffeur made way back to his mansion. Jewels wanted to see his baby brother more often, but his busy schedule would only permit so much time to spare. Nevertheless, it was good and refreshing to spend what little time he had to offer with his brother today. Turning his glass up to his lips, Jewels felt a hard bump in the rear. His liquor spilled all over his suit causing his anger to shoot sky high.

"What the fuck?!" he snapped. The driver quickly put the Maybach in park and jumped out to assess the damage. Jewels also exited the vehicle to make his fury known.

"I apologize," said the tiny man who was the reason for the accident.

"Apologize my ass, muthafucka! You see my suit and that bumper? I should kick your little ass all over these streets!" Jewels threatened.

The man pretended to be fake scared in order to buy time for the rest to show up. He silently tolerated Jewels disrespectful obscenities as an Astro van pulled up in front of the luxurious vehicle.

"Yo, boss? These clowns are blocking us in now," the chauffeur acknowledged.

Jewels turned around and was now headed in the opposite direction to deal with the matter. Unbeknownst to either of the unsuspecting men, the man responsible for the fender bender retrieved a taser from his jacket. Approaching the driver, he hit him in the neck with enough volts to drop him unconscious. Hearing the loud thump on the pavement, Jewels turned to find his man knocked out cold.

"What in the—" was all he managed to utter before three masked men leaped from the Astro van with assault rifles in hand.

Before Jewels could make a scene, he found himself bound, gagged, and in the trunk of his foreign wheels alongside his driver. It wasn't long before the two men were escorted to an apartment and separated.

"Whoever you niggas work for are dead men! I'm going to kill you, your mothers, fathers, sisters, brothers, and everybody you were ever associated with," Jewels vowed once the socks lodged in his throat were removed. Taking him into a bedroom, the leader of the kidnappers pushed him over onto the bed.

Removing his mask, he politely spoke, "Honey, let me tell you something right now. The only family I got is a man whom you've already took life from. As a matter of fact, I got a message for you from him," Sugar said. Pulling out a letter written by Cyrus, he began to read its contents to Jewels as the latter rolled over to face his attackers.

"Dear Jewels," Sugar began, "It's been a long time, old friend. When you crossed me and took away the only life I had as a free man, you killed me. You tried to bury me physically with your bullets but failed. Yet, even in my survival, you put me in an even far worse grave than I could ever have imagined. You forced me to live with the fact that I allowed you to kill Theo by not going with my first mind and staying by his side. I have to live with the fact that a 16-year-old kid never returned home to his mother because I allowed him to ride with us that night. God bless Johnny's soul. Well, today, vengeance is ours!"

Jewels couldn't believe his ears. He became quiet with fear, gripping his vocals as Sugar continued.

"When your little brother came in here, I knew that fate was smiling at me. Through him, I've watched your every move and knew that when the time was right, I would get pay back. Today, you will reap all that you've sown. As I have been forced to live with what I have wrought, so will you. Jewels, share my pain for a lifetime as you bleed like me... Sincerely, Cyrus," Sugar finished. Jewels watched as Sugar threw the letter down and pointed his phone at him.

"What are you doing?" he pleaded.

"Time to make a movie, baby," Sugar smiled.

The two goons unbuckled their belts and dropped their pants to the floor. Jewels began to scream so loud, they had to force the socks back into his mouth while raping him. Sugar recorded the entire gruesome scene on his iPhone. Once the men had their way with his bleeding anus, they got dressed and beat Jewels viciously. He could feel his bones breaking as they took aluminum bats to his body parts.

Pleased with the outcome, Sugar had one last move to make in order to seal the deal. Sugar had served time in prison for manslaughter. He had contracted AIDS from a cheating lover and killed him. With a syringe filled with his blood, Sugar stuck Jewels in the vein and shot it all in his system. Jewels laid covered in blood, semen, and sweat with tears in his eyes. He knew that his life would never be the same again.

Epilogue

Lil James, Derek, and Antonio's mouths were on the floor. Hood took the gun and tossed it on the bed in between them. "Well, I'm a man of my word, so now it's up to you guys," he said. The three boys looked at one another with a change of heart.

"Man, I ain't bout that life!" Lil James exclaimed.

"Yeah, I'm gucci on that shit," Antonio admitted.

Hood looked Derek square in his eyes. "What about you? You still want to go down that road?"

Derek picked up his pistol and handed it over to Hood. "Nah, my butt cheeks are sacred to me," he joked.

Hood couldn't help but laugh as he took the weapon away from the boys. "Good decision. I'm proud of y'all," Hood admitted.

"Thanks for giving us the real on how these streets get," Lil James replied.

"Whatever happened to Cyrus, Rodney, and Jewels, though?" Derek asked. Hood let out a sigh, indicating that the ending wasn't so happily ever after.

"Rodney got out of prison and Jewels blamed him for what happened. He killed his own brother. A few years later, he couldn't cope with living with the AIDS virus. He slit both of his wrists and died in his bathroom tub. Last, but not least, Cyrus was killed in a prison riot. The game is not a game. If you don't remember anything else, please remember that! Now, let's go and get some food and brainstorm about some legal ways to get paid," Hood said.

The boys all followed his lead out of the door. They were thankful for not going through with what could've eventually been the beginning of the end of their lives.

Deshion Hightower

Deshion Hightower aka Stack still incarnated after 28 years. I have changed my life and given it to God, family and friends. Thank you all for reading this and look out for more of me soon. Stay down!

Urban Aesop presents

A Pimp Bed

Deshion Hightower

Pimp Bed
A Short Story by
Deshion Hightower

The sky was blue, and the club was bumping with music from T.I. Stack was sitting in the cut by himself drinking a can of Bud Light. Club JB was always lit during the summer. Stack was looking at a text message from his partner Sano about a drug deal.

"Hey, Stack," said a voice he didn't recognize.

"Hey, Black. I haven't seen you in years. How you been doing, sexy?"

"I'm doing, fine," she said as Stack was admiring her beauty.

"So, what brings you to Cascade?" he asked, helping her with her seat.

"Well, my mother moved out as you know! She moved to North Druid Hills after she got out of rehab. I moved in to help watch over her and make sure she doesn't get to anymore drugs."

"Well, that's a great thing. She was going hard. Her and Miss Joyce was smoking like a pot of neck bones," Black said and giggled.

"I know and she's doing well, running her own business again."

"Good news! Tell her I said hey and God bless her."

"I will, Stack," he assured her.

Just then the bartender came over. "What would you like to drink?"

"Just a sprite, please," said Black.

"You sure you don't want nothing stronger?" he asked. That was peer pressure at it's finest , causing her to quickly folded.

"Ok, I'll have a rum and coke."

"Let me also get a rum and coke and a Cîroc with no ice," said Stack.

As they drank their liquor, Stack began to ask her lots of questions. "Do you remember when I use to try to talk to you and you always shot me down? I would wait on you when you came home at five o'clock. I would get your brief case and bags out of your car."

"Yes, I remember," said Black as she blushed. They both laughed at the fond memories of days gone by.

"Why you chumped me off like that?" he asked, suddenly serious.

"Because you were selling drugs. Plus my mom was buying them from you. I couldn't stand yo' lil ass."

Stack laughed at that. "I understand. I'm happy to hear that your mother is doing great and you are gorgeous, Ms. Lady."

"Thank you and thanks for my drinks, as well," she said as she flashed a smile at him.

"You are more than welcome, beautiful. Now, are you sure you can drive home?" he asked her slightly concerned.

"Yes, I will be fine," she said, shaking his hand before stood up to leave.

"So, are you leaving me a number?"

"Oh, sure," she said and before she could finish her sentence, Stack was already handing her his phone. After she put it in and took off to leave, he watched her as she walked away wearing a tight fitted dress that revealed all her curves. When he did, grabbed his dick.

"Damn, that motherfucker is fine," Stack mumbled. He then took off to drop a half a brick off to Sano. Sano gave him 8,000 cash, then they chopped it up for a while. He jumped in his truck and went to Harris's home for another game and played for two zips of cocaine.

***

Two weeks later, he and his partner Bias were sitting on a rental car drinking beer when a black car with bright lights pulled up real slow. They both went for their guns, thinking it was the police or the robbing crew. The lights went out and so did the car. That's when they saw a lady hopped out.

"Oh, shit. Black, you almost got busted," said Stack as put his gun away.

"Was y'all about to shoot me?" she asked with a shocked look on her face, not even knowing how close she was to death.

"Damn, you looking good tonight. Where are you headed?" Stack asked her, while pulling her close between his legs.

She looked at him and said, "I'm looking for you."

"Oh, well here I go."

She looked at Bais. "Well, daddy gotta come with me tonight. See ya."

Bais smiled at them both and shook his head.

Stack smelled liquor on her and he was drinking beer, so he knew she had been drinking heavily. She had on Louis Vuitton heels, shirt, and jeans. She was super fine in his eyes.

"Let me drive because I only had one beer."

"Ok, but it's a five speed."

"Ok, let's stop at the package store before it closes."

"I gotcha," he said as they pulled off.

After getting liquor, she told him to pull into a lot of houses he was very familiar with. It was plenty of drugs sold here.

"Hold on. Black, why are we stopping here?" he asked confused.

She looked at him and said, "Because this is where we are chilling at. This is my friend's house and nobody is here."

"Ok," he said and shrugged, following her.

They got out and went up the stairs into a patio door. When she opened the door, he put his hand on his gun. A waterbed was in the middle of the floor and mirrors were all around the wall. She kicked her heels off and quickly began to strip down to her panties and bra. He admired her body, her nice round ass, and titties.

"Wow," he whispered to himself.

They drunk liquor, talked, and got in the shower together. He was so hard, but she wouldn't let him do anything to her but wash her back. When it was her turn, she bathed him and dried him off.

"Why are you so long and hard?" she asked.

"That was a joke, right?" he said.

Black laughed and walked out of the bathroom. They were both naked sitting on the side of the bed when she spotted his gun.

"Why you got this?" she asked

"It's only for protection."

"Oh, I have a bigger one than this." She then went under the bed and came out with a 44 bulldog. She got up and went behind the mirror, then pulled a Glock out. He went to grab the gun from her, but she stopped him, motioning for him to hold on before she went in her Gucci bag and pulled a 45 out.

"I know how to work these, babies," she said as she pulled the trigger.

Boom!

Instantly, he fell backwards on the bed. It was silent. He couldn't hear anymore. All he could think of was, *this bitch tricked me and killed me.* After a couple of minutes, he felt something wrapped around his leg when his hearing came back. Black was screaming to God. He reached up and felt his head, realizing there was no blood. He sat up straight and looked down as she cried out in a rage. He then grabbed her and pulled her up on the bed beside him.

"It's okay. I'm not hit," he said as he tried to comfort her.

She looked at him. "I am so sorry. I don't know about guns. Get these away from me, please."

"I got them. Don't worry."

She was crying, snot was running from her nose. He got up, got her some tissue, then dried her face. "I am so sorry, Stack."

"I know. It's ok."

After a while, she calmed down and they drunk some liquor. Then had sex and fell asleep. All of a sudden, someone was banging on the door.

"I know you in there! Open the damn door," yelled a voice from the other side.

Stack opened his eyes and a light was shining through the window. He jumped out of the bed in a panic. "Who the fuck is that?" he asked as he grabbed his gun.

"That's my cousin's baby daddy," she said as she opened the door with the sheet wrapped around her.

"Man, you got to get out my crib ASAP!" It was a big guy who looked like a pimp.

Stack put his clothes in a hurry on while keeping his gun in his hand.. He then took off out the door and down the steps with her running behind him.

"Sorry, Stack. Let me give you a ride."

As they rode down to Cascade, she explained the situation about her cousin. She was with a guy who was her cousin's boyfriend/pimp. Stack learned never sleep in another man's bed.

The short story is called Pimp Bed.

***

Friday night, Micco called. "You ready?"

"Hell yeah. Jone, I'm ready," Stack said. He put on his bulletproof vest and stuck a 357 inside of it. Then he put his 45 in his waistline. Micco pulled up in an old Monte Carlo. They rode for thirty minutes, then got off the express way. They parked on a street behind the guy's house. They heard dogs barking when they got out.

Micco had a bag with cooked pork chops in it. He threw it on the ground and their dog ate it. They both jumped the fence and ran into the carport, lying down underneath. Stack was on Beecher Street late night, trapping his dimes of crack when a white caddy pulled up. The same big pimp looking guy from last night had a gun in his hand and was pointing it at Stack.

"Hey, lil nigga. Where my guns at?" asked the pimp.

"Brah, if you don't get that gun out my face, it's gonna be a real problem." he promised with an evil smirk.

"Oh, yeah? And what kind of problem is that?" By the time he got his last word out, he had a pistol to the back of his head.

"Fuck nigga, drop it or die," said Stack's cousin, Treeko. Of course, the pimp dropped the gun.

"Now, sucka. Where the money?" asked Treeko as he nudged him with the pistol.

"It's in the glove compartment," he whined like he hated to part with it.

His other cousin Torre went straight for the money and started to search the caddy. He came back with a duffel bag of drugs and a Kroger bag with money in it.

"Jackpot!" he said of the lick that came straight to them.

"Damn, you sweet pimp. Never come to another man's house and pull a gun. Now drive your bitch ass back to where you came from and hurry up," said Treeko. Pimp drove off fast not looking back. They spilt the money and drugs.

"Damn, that was a sweet lick. Nigga drove it right to us," said Torre as they all laughed.

Stack's partner Micco called him, asking did he want in on a lick. It was worth four bricks and lots of money. "Boy, speed that, cause I need that," he said.

"Ok, meet me at the spot Friday night round 1am."

"That's a bet, Jone," Stack told Micco and hung up. As he went to the trap to roll some more rocks, a fine ass junkie walked up.

"Hey, you got some more of that same stuff?" she asked and licked her lips like she could taste it. She was tall and thick in all the right places. Stack's dick got hard after looking at her fine ass.

"Yup, but first let me get some head," he said as he pulled his dick out. He got that top and shot off in her mouth. He then gave her two rocks and sent her on her way. He fired up a blunt sat on the couch and sold his dope untill a tap on the door awakened him. He clutched his pistol and opened his eyes. It was just another junkie wanting to buy some crack. After getting all his rocks off, it was time to go.

Stack put his presidential Rolex on after smoking a blunt of gas. He then put some Polo oil spray on, jumped in his truck and went to April's house. She came out with a dress and heels on with a beautiful hairdo.

He opened the passenger door for her and closed it as they drove to their destination. In the expensive restaurant they went to, she wanted a steak and broccoli while he ordered crab legs, shrimp, and a baked potato. They enjoyed the food, then went to the movies to see *Queen and Slim*. Later on, Stack hugged her in the parking lot, then caught her by surprise, kissing her slow and steady. She was loving it, too.

"So, do you want to go home with me tonight or something?" he asked, her hoping she'd say yes.

"No, I am afraid I can't this time, but you're a very kind gentleman. I thank you for the offer," she purred.

"Ok, maybe next time," he said with a chuckle.

"Yes, maybe next weekend, I should say," she said. What Stack did not know is she really wanted to go. The only thing holding her back tonight was her period. She then wished him a good night before she went into her house. He then drove off to handle a few things.

***

Stack was sitting in front of the store rolling a blunt when a crack head walked up to his window.

"Hey, bro. Lemme get a dollar," said the dark skin man. He had on a hoodie even though it was warm outside.

He knew it was some shit in the game, reaching for his pistol, but by time he grabbed his gun, the hoodie guy had shot through the window. Stack shot back and the guy took off running. He jumped out of the truck blasting his 45 at the man who fell down. People started screaming, coming out of the store running. He jumped in the truck and smashed out. He took a ride over to Jimmy's shop on Silver Road where Jimmy was working under a car.

"Hey, old man. Look at this," he said as he pointed at the truck.

"Dang, boy. Who tried to get you?" asked Jimmy as he looked at Stack.

"I don't know, unk. But fix it and paint it white. I will be back to get it in two weeks," he said as he gave Jimmy $2,000, then got in one of Jimmy rental cars.

****

"Man, some fool tried to shoot me through my window the other day," said Stack.

"What!" exclaimed Bais as he held the blunt between his lips. "Who was it, Jone?"

"Man, I don't know. But he might have gotten what he wanted. I don't know."

They both laughed.

***

Stack took his pit bull to Decatur. There figured there was a lot of money being placed on bets that day.. After he fed his dog a piece of raw meat and gave her some water, it was time for her to fight.

"Come on, girl. Let's get this win," he said. He went in his pocket, counted ten thousand in a hundred dollar bills, and gave it to the man that held the bets. He eyed the big dog his female dog had to fight.

"Damn, that's a big ass dog," he said, then got down on his knees and mumbled something into the dog's ear. His dog didn't budge but seemed to crack a smile. Both dogs then locked themselves together. The other guy's dog was very big and strong.

"Let's go, girl. Eat," he said as his dog ripped skin off the big pit's neck. Stack was urging her to fight. "Eat, baby. Eat."

The other dog was bleeding so badly, after ten minutes, they had to pull Stack's dog off of the big bleeding dog. Nobody else wanted to fight his dog that day, so he left with a smile on his face and winnings in his pocket. Back in the house, he cooked crack all night until he was done with everything he had.

This white chick name Cindy had called, saying her husband wanted to buy all the weight he had. He told her that he had seventeen pounds, and as long as her money was right, he would be on point. The deal was for Saturday night. He would surely have a couple killers with him when he meet them just in case they tried to catch him slipping. He promised himself that he would rob them if it came to it. It would be straight business. Nothing funny this time.

At the bar-b-que, it was a lot of dealing going on with his friends and people that he knew. Everyone was getting right. He stopped by the probation office and asked for April Lin.

The lady called to the back then said, "Go through those doors, sir and you will see Ms. Lin."

After waiting fifteen minutes, she finally came out. "Hey, I didn't know it was you," she said as he hugged her. "Come on in and have a seat. How did you find me?"

***

After a few days went by, Stack had moved out in Conyers, Georgia so he could duck off and stay out of the spotlight in Cascade for a while. His cousin Roe had told him about a lick that was worth a lot of money. He was thinking long and hard about it. It would be a big sting if they pull it off, so it was worth thinking about.

He got on his motorcycle and rode back to the hood in cascade to give his workers the bums of crack for the entire week he had already hid at the apartment building. After handing Kagg the backpack, he sped down town to the underground to meet April

They had met at the courthouse. When they did, she told him she was a probation officer. He was digging her. He pulled her seat out for her, and she thanked him. Then they ordered steak and potatoes. After talking with her for a while, he learned she was single and 31 years old. She also didn't want a guy that was crazy or in the streets

He was straight up with her, telling he'd been to jail nor was he completely out of streets yet, but planned to be soon. He could tell she was kinda square, but very clean and cool. That made him want her more. When their date was over, he followed her home on his bike to make sure she made it home safely. Afterwards, he got a long wet kiss from her and left.

***

They were headed into the house that had all the dope and money in it. Five of them surrounded the house with AK 47s. Stack and Toby kicked the front door in, shots starting to ring everywhere. They both hit the ground. Micco and Roe had kick the back door in with Treeko coming in from an upstairs window. They all ducked behind sofas and whatever they could find. There were two shooters in the kitchen just blasting away. They were all trapped with nowhere to run. When the shooting stopped in the kitchen, they all ran in on the guys.

"Get ya ass down!" yelled Stack.

The two guys' ammo had ran out. They drugged the two white men in hopes of getting what they wanted.

"Ok, bitch. Where the money and dope or die tonight?" said Roe as he bust the tall guy across the head with pistol hard as hard as he could. The guy started to point at the wall bleeding badly.

"Get up, bitch!" yelled Roe.

The guy got on his knees and pulled the sheet rock up. When he did, everyone's eyes shined brightly at all the drugs they saw. It was all meth and there was a small bag full of hundreds. They then tied the guys up and searched the house. They found lots of jewelry and money left headed for Fulton County.

***

Stack and his crew pulled up in a big black truck. After an hour went by, the door opened and a lady came out. Micco slid from out of the car and Stack followed suit as Micco grabbed the lady from behind.

"Shhh, don't say anything," he said as he walked her in front of him through the house. "Who else in here?" he whispered.

She shook her head nobody. Stack cased the house out with both guns in hand.

"Okay, if you want to live give me all the money and dope," said Micco.

She shook her head "yes" as she pointed at the freezer.

"Okay, get it out," he growled. She went in the deep freezer and came out with two bags of white powder. Then she pulled out two more bags of white powder.

"Nah, this ain't all of it," said Stack as he put the gun to her back. "Come on. We want all of it."

She took them upstairs and requested for them to help her move the bed. They obliged as she got on her knees and pulled the carpet up and a built in safe was there. They smiled at each other. She opened it up and stacks of hundreds were revealed. They watched her fill the duffel bags up. When she was done, they tied her up with a sheet so she could get herself loose in at least ten minutes. That way they could get a head start to get away since they didn't want to hurt her.

"That's everything, y'all," said Stack.

Micco put duct tape on her mouth and went to her camera, busting it on the floor. He got the DVD before they fled out the front door.

"This shit was to easy, Jone. I'm retiring," said Stack as they both laughed and rode home.

***

"Well, I followed you one day," he said as he sat across from her.

She busted out laughing. "Hold on, sir. Didn't I tell you I didn't want a crazy guy?"

"Yeah, but I'm not crazy," he said and smiled at her.

"Well, are you stalking me?" she said and dared him to deny it.

"No, I just wanted to see where my woman works," he said, making a day, as well.

"Well, I didn't know we were together already," she said as a smile played against her lips.

"Yes, we are officially an item," he proclaimed as if were a new law.

"Okay, I guess we are then," she said and shrugged since she had no problems with it.

"So, are we eating tonight?"

"I got something you can eat," she said, smiling.

"Okay. What time will I be picking you up?" he asked.

"About eight, sir," she laughed.

"Okay, ma'am," he said as he got up to leave.

He stopped by the gas station to fill up, making sure the handle of his gun. He wanted to could grab it in case something was fishy. He really didn't know what was going on since the dude shot through his window. He had to be extra cautious from now on. After he took April to dinner, he went to her house where they made love for hours.

He didn't wake up until 3PM the next day. After he got up, he went to drop his mother and grandparents down a few thousands a piece. While he was there, he ate dinner with his grandfather, then slid out the back door to his car.

He put on all black then met up with the crew, then they rode to Sandy Springs, Georgia. They went to a hotel where everyone got a few hours of sleep. At 5AM, Sano woke them up.

"Let's do it, boys. Money is time," he said. He explained that it was a guy who owned jewelry stores. He had lots of jewelry and gun cases in his home, so there was no telling what else was in there. "He;s leaving at 5:45. I did my homework. Now he has alarms, so we got to cut the wires, then go in the back door."

Stack and Micco cut the wires, opened the window, and slid through. They opened everything up, looking around and checking the house to make sure it was clear.

"Jackpot," said Bais as he found the cases of jewelry.

"Jackpot," said Micco as he found a black bag full of diamonds.

They all started bagging up guns. There were so many, they couldn't get them all. After they split up everything, everyone went their own ways. As Stack looked through his bag of jewelry and diamonds, he found a ring for his mom and grandma. April had told him that her favorite color was purple. In the bag, there was a ring that cost $15,000.

When he saw it, he didn't even think twice. He just knew she was the one. *This is hers,* he thought to himself as he walked to Jessie's store. There, he bought an orange juice and stopped at Mr. JB's club to chat with the OG for a while. Mr. JB wanted to spend three stacks on diamonds so he would be back with them ASAP.

Stay Tuned!

The full version of "Pimp Bed" will be coming soon from Urban Aesop Publications.

Billie Miff

As Urban Relationship author's jockey for a leading position on the bestsellers list, Billie Miff would rather be your number one choice when it comes to a good, mature novel filled with realistic situations. Each chapter in each story, takes on a life of its own, drawing the readers in, up close and personal with the characters. Fiction blends with reality when Billie Miff takes you on a journey. A page turned and a lesson learned. There's always something special inside each classic material.

PG 13: Prince Georges Finest
A Short Story by
Adam Upperman

Chapter 1

"Bro, you don't have to do this!" Kash whimpered, while staring at the death end of the 9mm. The black hole looked menacing from that angle, as if it were one eye giving one last look at his existence. He gulped once, then his voice changed an octave. "Damn, things were all good just a week ago."

Kash gave Stash a weak smile that seemed to infuriate him even more. There were some things you didn't joke about, some things he couldn't just let go. Some things that couldn't just change once they're done.

"Kash, you can save your Jay-Z lines for the mix tape. In fact, you should really get some new material ready. Where you're going, they'll be looking for some hot shit! Get it? " Stash had to laugh at himself in his attempt at sarcasm. He knew Kash probably wasn't in the mood for humor with the barrel of a gun pointed directly at his forehead, but hey, that was the bed he made. Now he's got to lie in it.

Speaking of lies, that's how Kash got into this predicament in the first place. All he had to do was keep it one hundred with Stash from the jump. He was the one who always had Kash back. When the heat came down on him, it was Stash who jumped into the fire with him and pulled him out.

It was Stash who made allowances for his fuck-ups, then smoothed it over with the rest of the crew. But to have someone close to him lie? Now that's the first sign of disloyalty and the ultimate betrayal. And if he were to tolerate it one more time, then the door would be open for anyone else in the crew to test his gangsta.

"You lying to me, Kash, is something I just can't have," Stash said, gritting his words through clenched teeth.

"Its not what it looks like, bro," Kash said as he tried to plead his case they way someone who is in the wrong does.

"So you didn't lie to me about you and your boys pulling a job without us?" He didn't know that I already had my answers.

"Well, yes, but I can explain that," he said, putting his hands up in the air in defense.

"Put your fuckin' hands down before I make them nubs. Now your so-called boys aren't really as close to you as you think. They're the ones who tipped me to your little clandestine activities. And furthermore, I heard that they weren't all the way down with your plan. They even told you at you stand to collect more by sticking with us, your crew, your family. But when they tried to warn you, your greedy ass said fuck me and came up with a master plan. What was your master plan, Kash?" Stash asked, letting one shot go to the ground right between his legs.

The blast echoed off the walls of the abandoned warehouse. Stash had lured Kash there with some news of them partnering up to pull off a very lucrative heist. It was worth a few hundred thousand. Stash knew his greedy ambition couldn't resist the opportunity.

"C'mon, let me hear it." By now, Kash was shaking uncontrollably. He didn't know what to say because there was no right answer. Stash wondered what could he say to clean up the mess he had made.

"Stash, me and the others, we're like family to you. We've been through a lot together and made some good money, too!"

Kash made him remember the good times when they skillfully put a job together from scratch, carefully planned it out and assigned duties. Everyone played a role, then got it pulled off to perfection. They'd meet up at the safe house, laugh about near misses, drink a little, smoke a little, split our earnings then go our separate ways. That was how they got down—the PG13. They belonged to each other, no love for those outside our crew.

The only way they survived was through trust. Each detail of each job had its own set of consequences, one relying on the other. Like the bank job they did over in Laurel. It was a busy Monday, midday when traffic was bustling. They picked that day because that particular branch made their drop at the close of business on Mondays. Their intel gave them accurate inside information that would be vital to their success.

Their girl Numb, short for Numbers, was on point as usual.

"There are six cameras total at this Signature Trust and Loan. One facing the parking lot, two pointing at the entrance, two at the tellers, and one more over the vault. They employ two security guards, one by the door and another at floats around. There are a total of eight tellers. An Asian woman, one black male, two white females, middle-aged and damn near elderly, one black female with trust issues, one pregnant Hispanic, a Vietnamese male with a bad toupee, and a young, white male who we assume to be the supervisor. He's the one who moves the money from the drawers to the money bags."

Stash absolutely loved Numb's attention to detail. With her research and their man Guap, AKA Richard Campbell, on the inside, their operation was nearly in the bag, no pun intended. When they were ready to strike, it would be a quick hit. Their target was to grab no less than $250k. A bank that size generated a nice cash flow mainly because of its location and Saturday banking. That worked in their favor, that and the fact it was easily accessible to the Beltway.

They pulled up in two nondescript sedans with tinted windows. Speedy and Stick were the two drivers they always used to make the cleanest and expedient getaways. They never failed them and Stash never failed to pay them their worth. The night before, Spider, their Puerto Rican night crawler, worked his magic by blackening out the outside camera. He also mapped out their easiest means of escape.

When they jumped out, everything was clean. Their business suits were neatly fitted, weapons were concealed, and retractable duffel bags were tucked in the smalls of their backs. Nothing looked suspicious. Rolex, their timekeeper, set her watch as they stepped inside. Hardly anyone noticed the clear masks over their faces as they busied about. By the time the roaming security guard realized something was wrong, it was too late.

"Get on the floor and nobody gets hurt," Sandman growled at the security guard in a low but firm tone.

He was a burley guy, muscles barely being contained by the suits' material. Before the guard could respond, he was hit with some sort of spray concocted to put any victim to sleep. Simultaneously, Nottz did the same to the other guard. Sandman and Nottz were the muscle with Nottz being the more aggressive of the two. For this job, they needed his kinder, gentler side. The last thing they needed was a body count, which is what he was known for.

By the time Stash got to the counter, he already saw Sasha spring into action. She had the white boy supervisor so engrossed in her cleavage that he never figured he would be the next victim of the sleeping potion. It was time for phase two.

"Everybody remain calm. This will be over with before you know it," Stash announced. "Do not, I repeat do not try to be a hero. Heroes have their place in the graveyard. We are not here to take any lives, just a little bit of this money." He looked and motioned to Nottz. "You and number two, hold down the floor out here. Three and four, you come with me."

He assigned everyone numbers to keep the names off the airways. Order always breeds success.

"This fine young man is going to direct us to the unmarked, undied bills." As Guap moved nervously towards the back, which was all rehearsed, a quick movement caught Stash's eye. "Hey, you! With the bad hair!" The Vietnamese man froze in his tracks like he didn't do anything. He shot a blast from his pistol the man's direction, taking out the screen on the computer to get his attention. "Get your ass out here! In fact, all y'all back there come to the front. Five, keep an eye on these folks," he said. Sasha nodded. "Six, what's the time looking like?"

"Three minutes, boss. And we gotta be outta here."

"You heard that! Let's wrap this up!"

They came out of there with four duffel bags full of one hundreds, fifties and twenties. Speedy and Stick pulled up as we exited. No one was harmed, a job well done. On their way out and just for good measure, Sasha sprayed Guap and put him down. She would have to apologize to him later for that. He would meet up with them at the point and get his cut for being a good soldier. They made it to the switch point where they dumped the two getaway cars and hopped in the Mercedes conversion van driven by Dozier.

Their team was mean, clean, precise, professional, and most of all, loyal. There was enough money to go around and there was always the next job, so greed should never have been an issue. He figured maybe it wasn't about greed that made Kash turn. Maybe it was power. Some guys couldn't stand to see another man in control. But what Kash failed to realize is with leadership comes great responsibility.

Everyone in the crew was hand picked, including him, and everyone had a role to play. How effective they played that role was Stash's responsibility. He didn't choose this life. This life chose him the same way he was chosen. Thinking is a vital part of the game and Kash couldn't have been thinking when he chose to cross him. Whoever influenced his decision, steered him wrong.

He would soon pay for getting to Stash's man and twisting his head. He had a good idea who it was, so maybe he would spare the rest of them since a couple of them did tip him off to his crooked ass. He just had to see what kind of mood he would be in when that day came. Today, however, he had a fish in the pan that needed to be fried.

"Kash, Kash, Kash, you're right. We have been through a lot together. Some good times, some bad, some high, some low. This, my man, is definitely a low time for us. The sad part about it is you haven't just destroyed our trust, but the others, as well."

"What you don't know, Stash, is that some of them was looking to flip on you, too," he managed to say in a low tone, then gave him a slight smirk. With the handle of the pistol, Stash drew back and smashed it across his jaw, instantly causing blood to trickle from his lip.

"Don't you dare try and include my loyal soldiers into your mess. The same hole you dug for yourself, you gonna be buried in it." The look that he gave him told it all. Stash was through talking.

"C'mon, man. Stash and Kash, we ride together or die together." He gave Stash one last glimmering look, hopping to spark some sympathy. It didn't do nothing but spark his rage as he cocked back the hammer and let it boom.

"We did ride together, but you must die alone."

Chapter 2: The Chasers

Speedy popped the clutch and switched gears like he was driving at the Audubon in Germany. He was dashing in and out of lanes on the Beltway trying his best to elude the Maryland State troopers. Montgomery County police radioed ahead and alerted them that a charcoal grey Jaguar was seen leaving an upscale neighborhood where a breaking and entering was reported. He called ahead and told his partner-n-drive, Stick, to meet him at the New Carrolton metro train station. He needed him to be ready with his Audi. He had some police to shake.

By the time Speedy reached the Prince George's County sign on the Beltway, there was already a full-scale, high-speed chase in progress. The Prince George cops were sure to pick up pursuit once he excited the highway. He had to think fast because the two state troopers were hanging tough, sirens blaring with the lead car barking commands to the other cars and to Speedy. The other cars complied as best they could in the mild rush hour traffic. In the DC metro area, anytime after 4pm weekdays, they were subject to be in heavy traffic flow bordering gridlock.

The sleek Jaguar swerved in and out of lanes at a speed nearing the triple digits. Speedy was under complete control. He was built for this type of intense driving, yet he needed a diversion—something to slow them down a bit. As always, he had a plan.

He hit the conference mode on his phone and dialed up Sasha and Numbers. Now those two girls were fierce drivers in their own right. Its just that everybody has a role to play. Stash wanted Speedy, Stick, and Dozier to do the driving. He had other plans for the girls. Had Stash seen them in action, he may have had a change of heart.

"Hey, girls. I'm in a bit of a jam and need your help."

"Where you at?" Numbers asked.

"Yeah, I hear a bunch of noise like you're shifting gears," Sasha remarked

He calmly answered, "Actually, I am. I'm in a high speed chase with the state troopers behind me."

"What! Speedy, what did you do?" Sasha had concern in her tone.

"Nothing. Just a mistake in identity. Don't worry, I have a plan. Remember when I gave you guys a hard time about buying the same style and color Jaguar that I have?"

"Yup," Sasha quipped. "You were pissed with us something serious. I mean really in your feelings."

"Purely a coincidence," Numbers added.

"Point taken. Listen, I need you guys to meet me on the Beltway in those cars. I'll explain what to do when you get in motion."

"This is gonna cost you, Speedy. I was just about to sit down to some grilled salmon." Sasha was dead serious.

"How do we catch up with you? Aren't you already on the Beltway?"

"Yup, I just came by the Silver Spring exit, leaving out of Montgomery County."

"Oh, so you're heading north?"

"He's coming our way, so if we leave now, we should meet up," Numbers figured

"Either we will meet up or you may be just behind me. The plan will work both ways." Speedy could see the wheels turning.

"We got you, partner. Just remember, you'll owe us both a salmon dinner at the restaurant of our choice when this is over," Sasha bargained.

"Deal." Speedy popped the clutch, then pulled off from the pursuing police. Their sirens blared loud enough to alarm other drivers, causing them to slow down and pull over, giving the chasers a straight shot last their target.

He weaved in and out, tires squealing as he passed the slowing cars. Exits became a blur as he gained speeds close to 90mph. This wasn't even close to the Jag's full potential. Speedy then phoned his partner Stick.

"There's been a change of plans, bro. They're tailing me too close and I won't be able to make that move at the train station. I've got another idea, though. Head towards the safe house and I'll call you back."

As soon as he hung up from Stick, he could see the twin Jaguars up ahead. A smile crept across his face.

"I see you guys. Just keep it at that pace. I'm gonna pull up to you in a few seconds. We're gonna play a little game of three card Monty with these cops."

"I like the sound of that!" Numbers shrieked out with excitement. She loved games that involved numbers.

The state troopers were indeed in for a mind game. As the chase ensued, their numbers increased. A few more cars soon flowed onto the highway from neighboring exits. What they didn't know was Speedy and the girls had a couple of tricks up their sleeves.

The Jaguars were not just identical, but were custom built and manufactured in Europe, so they still had the foreign style license plates. The only difference was these were able to change into James Bond style. They were highly illegal in the states, but this crew hardly played by any rules.

"Pull over to the shoulder!" fhe command came through the air from the trailing trooper. The state had these troopers equipped with Dodge Challengers that were souped up so they could keep up with high performance vehicles. It also gave them lasted egos, ones that needed to be shrunk down to size.

The Maryland State Troopers have been the enemy of the criminal state for years. There was a time in the early 90s when the highways weren't waste to drive on without fearing for you life. In fact, in recent times kings have gotten worse for the commuter. One instance to date was a man of Somalian descent, traveling on the Beltway. He was headed home to Alexandria, Virginia, traveling with his wife and young daughter. It was one of those muggy summer afternoons heading towards evening. It was right after rush hour where the sun hadn't yet set.

The air in the metro area can be pick with humidity in the summertime, so it wasn't uncommon for cars to roll on the highway with their windows down, especially those cars without the luxury of AC. Ali and his family were one of unfortunate travelers suffering from the sweltering heat.

During their commute, an insect made its way inside the vehicle exciting the young girl in the backseat. Being the protective father that he was, Ali tried his best to shoo the flying bug away from his daughter. At an opportune moment, he swerved moved violently into a vacant lane with no harm to anyone.

He regained control, but not before the eyes of the law had caught him. For the state trooper was in the median lurking for any suspicious activity, this made his day. He quickly got behind Ali and threw his lights on, ordering him to pull over to the shoulder. Without hesitation, Ali complied.

"License and registration!" sas all the expressionless officer commanded

"Sir, may I explain my position?" Ali asked in his thick American accent.

"So, you admit to doing something wrong, huh?"

"No, sir. I was merely—" he started to say before he could finish.

"Which one is it? Did you or did you not swerve into that lane back there?" he questioned again.

"Well, yes but there was—" he said, but cut short again.

"Get out of the car!"

"Sir, I don't think that's necessary. If I could explain."

"Get out of car, now! I think I need to do a sobriety test on you. Don't you think it's a little early to be drinking. I swear you foreigners think you can do whatever you want. I'm gonna show you today who's the boss in the country."

"Mr. B..." Ali tried to read his name and get his badge number but the officer quickly covered it up. In the process, he turned off his body camera used for instances just like that.

"Move!" he demanded, snatching Ali by the arm and taking him the back of the car.

"C'mon with the test. Anything you have, I will pass it. Then you will see that I am not drunk," Ali said boldly

"Shut up! You don't make any demands around here."

The officer took Ali's license to his squad car, then returned as quickly as he left. "Here!" He threw Ali's ID at him, which bounced off his chest and then to the ground. This infuriated Ali. The disrespect was an insult to his culture.

"Pick that up!" Ali demanded.

" What?" the officer asked. He was taken aback by Ali's bold order.

"You heard me. Pick it up and hand it to me the same way I gave it to you. Respect me as a man."

"You don't deserve respect, foreigner." That remark triggered a switch in Ali, causing him to lose focus as to where he was. He bent down to retrieve his license, then cane up with a swift blow straight to the officer's groin area causing him to double over in pain.

"Agghh! You motherfucker!" the officer howled out.

Ali scurried past him trying to make it to the car door so he could flee the scene. He never was able to reach the driver's side door handle.

Pop! Pop! Pop! Pop! The sound heard that filled the thick air.

"My God, no!" Ali's wife shrilled from the car.

"Daddy!" his daughter cried out as Ali's body slumped to the ground. Their cries were drowned out by the officers's siren blaring as he sped away from the bloody scene. The murder in broad daylight is still considered an cold case. No one stepped up to state what they saw that day. A harmless insect and what should've been a routine traffic stop turned into a man losing his life due to an overly aggressive, prejudiced, renegade state trooper.

So Speedy and his crew were well aware of the dangers on the Maryland highways. That's why stopping to explain was a mistake in identity would not keep him safe. Doing what comes natural always kept him safe, driving fast.

"I see y'all. Make some space. I'm gonna pull in between you two."

They all slowed down to allow the chasing vehicles a close enough distance to feel like they've made up ground, then simultaneously, all three Jags increased their speed. The road opened up, most of the traffic now clear to the shoulder or median. Some of the drivers even stood outside their cars with their phones on recording the show. For some, it was like watching NASCAR. Let the games begin!

Sasha slowed down, allowing Speedy to lead. Numbers sped up and got in front, then quickly broke off the formation, making it appear like it did before except the positions had changed. Speedy was now on the left, Numbers was in the middle, and Sasha was in the right lane.

"Middle car, pull over to the shoulder now!" the squawking radioed ordered.

They switched the formation again, just as easy as they did the first time. This time Numbers was on the right and Sasha was in the middle, while Speedy stayed in the same lane. Their plates changed as they changed, so the troopers couldn't get a clear read on who was who.

"Okay, girls. Let's give these cops a real show." Speedy to took the lead with the other two in tow, forming a straight line. They moved like that, switching lanes at speeds topping 100mph. For the audience that had formed, it was quite a show.

"And for the grand finale!" he yelled as he opened his sunroof, then pulled out a neatly wrapped stacks of bills out of the console. He freed the hundreds from their paper restriction, then tossed them through the hole in the roof, letting the air create a rain storm.

"Ha, ha! Money ain't a thang!" he hollered out.

The falling money caused the onlookers who manned their phones to go and chase the gifts from heaven. Never mind the fact they could potentially be hit by the speeding troopers. Free money was accumulating in the street and this didn't happen everyday. People were trying to grab as much as they could out of the air, some even ran out into oncoming traffic to collect, others followed like fools. The state troopers blew their horns to move the pedestrians, but to no avail. The money overruled all judgment. The troopers' pursuit had haulted. Speedy and the girls took the next exit and disappeared out of sight. Just another day in the life of being on the other side of the law.

Chapter 3 : The Meeting

"Here you go, gentlemen," the voluptuous waitress said as she served their drinks, bending over just enough to give them an eyeful of her cleavage. A trick she learned long ago. She knew how to entice men into giving up handsome tips. This crew had been tipping all night, so she was definitely on her game.

"Hold on, sweetheart. We didn't order these," Castro said as he made an attempt to push the tray back.

"Oh, these come courtesy of those ladies over there. Now if you want, I can send them back." One of the ladies raised her glass as if to toast to their acquaintance long distance. Once Castro saw how beautiful she was, he reconsidered.

"No, I believe we will indulge. Don't want to be disrespectful. Right, fellas?" he asked almost rhetorically, knowing their greedy asses would agree to anything free.

"Okay, you guys enjoy, but not too much. I am the jealous type," she said, throwing a wink at Castro with her long lashed eye.

As soon as she was out of ear shot, Castro boasted, "I told y'all the strip club is where the bitches is at!"

"Yeah, you got them sending drinks our way and everything."

"You heard that waitress, big homie. She is jealous of those women over there," one of Castro's cronies commented.

"Oh, just that's just tip talk. The kind of stuff you say when you want your customers to dig deep in their pockets."

"Well, whoever that woman is who sent the drinks, obviously likes you because she's on her way over here." Castro looked up and tried to compose himself, more so to keep his boys from knowing he was a bit nervous.

Before he got himself together, her gaze was upon him like a cheetah on a defenseless gazelle. She was the most stunning woman he had ever seen. He had had some women in his day being a well-known local entrepreneur, but rarely to they have the boldness of this one who definitely knews what she wanted. Castro was in her sights.

Frederick Cassius came from Dominican roots but always considered himself a member of the African American community. When his family moved to the DC metro area, he adopted the moniker, Castro, because he admired the powerful leader Fidel Castro. So much so, he vowed to have the kind of success that could run DC. He dreamed big and worked hard to make his dreams comes true. He wanted those around him to enjoy life, winning last all costs.

Young Freddie Castro had a hustler's ambition early on and things seem to fall his way. Old heads took a liking to him and gave him the game. He was taught how to shoot glocks and AKs before he could even shoot a good cum load in a hottie. That was fine with him because he was also taught the importance of money over bitches. The basic lessons of street philosophy he learned from hood professors and legends. He earned his stripes by pulling jobs and it didnt take long before he graduated with honors.

Soon Freddie Castro put his own crew together. These were some loyal boys built to do his bidding. The good thing about them was that they were down to do the dirty work and any leader needed some guys to do that. They never questioned his authority. He took care of them for their efforts. When there was a drop to be made, they did it. Trips out of town to handle business were easily completed by his workers voluntarily. That made it easier to build his mini empire.

Castro learned how to network from watching and listening to the OGs. He soaked up the knowledge, then inherited a few connects just by being loyal himself. These connections turned out to be the jump start he needed. He took Sir advice and started slow, but it didn't take long for things to blossom.

Two of his major ventures were outside of the District—one in New York, the other down south in Georgia. Castro would get a few kilos of the purest cocaine from a prosperous dealer in Queens for a cheap price, then turn a mean profit down in the metro by bassing it up. The monies made off the coke distribution, he would send south with his men who would meet his arms dealer.

The dealer would buy the latest guns from the Georgia gun shows they ran monthly, then send them back up north by car or bus. They would get them in DC, keep the ones they wished to use and move the remainder on up to New York where they went for the high high. New Yorkers would pay top dollar for quality weapons, especially brand new.

His profits from these ventures allowed him to expand his business in more legal ways like real estate and a car dealership. Castro had a plan and his game in tact. He just had one flaw—he was a sucker for beguiling women.

"So what you guys got planned for tonight?" the alluring woman who sent the drinks asked seductively.

"We haven't decided yet, " Castro responded in his smooth baritone. "What you want to get into? I can ditch these guys and it can just be me and you," he offered, totally disregarding the guys who were loyal to him. A couple of dudes at the table looked on in astonishment at just how quickly their leader had dissed them. What was to be expected? There were four of them and only one of her.

"Don't leave me out," the voluptuous waitress walked by, overhearing the night plans being made. The first woman was kind of taken by surprise by the woman's forwardness. Woman can be catty, as she gave her a look of discontent but didn't say anything. It was obvious she had a plan and it was just interfered with.

"Shoot, we can make a party of this," he said as Castro's eyes lit up like high beams. His boys saw a glimmer of hope that their night may have took a turn for the better but was quickly extinguished by Castro's greed for woman. " The three of us can get into some thangs," he countered. The two women looked at each other, then smiled.

They left the club as a group but separated once outside. Castro and his two dates jumped in his Maserati, while his boys sped off in an Expedition heading in the other direction.

"I didn't catch either of y'all names, " he asked as he caught their eyes in the rear view mirror. Castro had them both in the back seat. He had a thing about having people he didn't know in his passenger seat. Biggie and Tupac had taught him that the passenger seat was a dangerous spot to be in.

"I'm Angel Dust, but you can call me Angel," the voluptuous one said and winked.

"Angel Dust? Whoa! How did you get that name, if I may ask?"

"Well, put it this way. Once you sprinkle me on anything, you're hooked like an addict."

"Alright, now!" he boomed out. The other sucked air through her teeth at the woman's attempt at sounding seductive. To her, it sounded like an lame line. "And your name?" Castro asked, noticing she had just ended a call.

"Oh, I'm Shyanne. Pleasure to meet you, big spender."

"Please, just Castro or you can call me Freddie once we get more personal. I'm hoping that's the plan for tonight."

"If you play your cards right," Angel said, leaning forward so he knew it was her that was being the aggressor.

"You sure making a lot of calls back there, Shyanne. Are we not being good company for you?" Castro jested.

"Well, if you must know, I had to clear some things up with my husband since I'll be out late. That's not a problem, is it?" she shot back.

"Oooooh, Angel. We have one breaking the rules. Hey, Shyanne. I don't have a problem with what you do, but whoever was on the other end of that call may have the problem. What you think about that, Angel?" It was getting under her skin how he kept trying to get validation from the skank next to her.

"We're not gonna get you in any trouble are we, sweetheart?" Angel whispered

"Trouble? No, none for me. I'm good." Shyanne's confident stare seemed to quiet them for a second.

"Well, then, we're in for an event filled evening. How about my place? I have a condo in Greenbelt," he boasted

"Sounds like a plan," she said.

That fit right into what Shyanne had in mind. Shyanne was really Sasha. She had been targeting Castro at the club. In fact, she had been on assignment for the past few weeks. Whether tailing him to the bank watching him make deposits or listening in on his calls while he conducted business at local restaurants. She was ever so close to obtaining the details to a big payday.

Sending the drinks to his table was her way of sealing their connection for the night. She had no clue there would be a third party. This Angel chick had come out of nowhere and foiled the initial plan but Shyanne proved to be more savvy. She would never let on what her end game entailed.

Stash had meticulously planned this mission for his number one girl and would not be denied. The rest of he team was in position. All she had to do was give the "GO" call. The tracker on her phone that was activated at the club was enough to get a read on her current location. Dozier and the demolition boys were already en route and should be meeting up with the vehicle in a matter of minutes. Stick and Numbers would serve as back up.

Coming out of the District, Castro had to take residential streets to get to his home. He was so thrilled and anxious to be in the company of two sexy ladies, he couldn't stop smiling. All he could think about was the stories he would brag about to his crew.

Shyanne continued to glance down at her phone to make sure the locator was still blinking. Angel was making a lot of small talk, so nothing seemed conspicuous. The conversation shifted and Castro asked

Shyanne some general questions trying to feel her out. She kept her composure and answered all his inquiries with short, brief replies. She wasn't there to make new friends, surely not in the form of Freddie Castro. In her eyes, he was the enemy. Stash made sure she knew that. She was to stay focused on the agenda because there was a lot at stake.

"I can't believe it!" Castro said as he banged his hand on the steering wheel in frustration. "Construction at this hour of the night?" There were workers with orange reflector vests directing traffic around the work area.

All of a sudden, out of nowhere, an old school van with a primed up paint job came barreling through the intersection, crashing into Castro's foreign car. The passenger side front wheel crumpled in like aluminum foil. Castro was dazed by the collision. It took a moment for him to come to his senses.

"Oh, hell no! I know these muthafuckas didn't just wreck my Mozzy!" he cried out, ignoring the blood trickling from his forehead. He climbed out trying to regain his balance, then assessed the damage. The girls got out too, checking themselves for any injuries. Castro was so engrossed in the inspection of his car, he never noticed the two masked men draw down on him.

"Come go with us!" Castro quickly realized they had the drop on him, so he threw his hands up. Things started to make sense a he gave the girl, Angel, a menacing stare.

"You. I should've remembered that birthmark on your lip. You changed your hair but you had the one at my spot last month."

"Shut that shit up! This ain't about no bitch! Now let's go!" Castro then redirected his anger at the assailants.

"I ain't going no muthafuckin where! Not after what you did to my ride!"

One of the men didn't take kindly to his smart mouth, catching him across the jaw with the butt of his block. Blood poured from his mouth, then things went dark in his world. The other man put a cloak over his head, then shoved him in the van.

"Hey, where are you taking him?" Angel shouted out.

"What's it mean to you?" Sasha asked. Angel was fidgety while reaching in her purse. Sasha's street smarts saw the move coming a mile away, having her gun already cocked and ready. They stared at each other before any words were exchanged. "Why are you so concerned about this? You're just a strip club waitress trying to get some cheap thrills," Sasha said, her words meant to be an insult.

"He's my mark. I had plans to work him for cash. It was working too, until you decided to cock block with the old "send the drinks" move!" Angel fired back.

"Cock block? Bitch, we've been on him for weeks. Just waiting on the time to jump down and tonight is the night."

"Well, tonight was the night for me, too, "Angel replied.

"So now what?" Sasha powered up. "You gonna leave us to our business?"

"You ain't the only bitch with a gun here," Angel shot back, hers pointed in Sasha's direction

"That's right! She ain't the only one!" Numbers said, jumping out of Stick's Porsche, two guns ready to blaze. "This bitch don't play no games. I do addition by subtraction." Angel realized quickly that she was outnumbered, throwing her hands up in submission.

"You may feel like you have the upper hand but actually, we need each other."

"Oh yeah? How's that?" Sasha quipped.

"Well, I'm assuming you and your crew are making a money play," Angel spoke calmly

"And if we are?" Numbers interjected.

"The real treasure is at his house. Unless you're gonna bully it out of him, he's not gonna just walk you in."

"So what are you getting at?" Sasha was growing impatient but was willing to see what her bargaining chip was.

"I've been there. You heard him. I know where he lives, know the code to get in. I even know where the stash is...plus more."

"How do we know you not bluffing?" Numbers asked, not trusting a soul.

"You get nothing if you don't trust me, but stand to gain a lot if we work together."

Sasha looked at Numbers, then back at Angel. They all had to admit, she made a hell of a point. All they planned had to be reconsidered.

Chapter 4: Teaming Up

They all got in cars and headed to their destination. Angel gave directions in the lead car, Dozier trailing them in the van that held the hooded Castro. He had no idea what was going on or what was about to happen. Sasha had to regroup. She was given instructions to carry out and one more person had completely changed things. The worst part about it was she had to report the change back to Stash. He always wanted a progress report on missions he wasn't directly involved in.

"What's going on out there? Dozier mentioned a problem at the pick up spot?" Sasha didn't have a chance to give her version because Dozier already alerted him to a problem. Stash still wanted answers, good or bad. The way he operated, he generally always had the solution but wanted to see how it would play out. He's a smart man and a genuinely good leader, so it was hard to get over on him. He didn't take no shit.

"It appears that another woman had the same idea as we did. Purely coincidence," Sasha explained.

"And who is this woman?" Stash asked, now curious.

"She says her name is Angel Dust. She's a waitress at the club where we picked up Castro. She claims to have already targeted Castro." Sasha spoke loud enough for Angel to hear, no longer having any concern. It was her operation to see through and she would not let her boss down.

"Is she there with you?" Stash asked

"Yes, she is." Sasha looked Angel in the eye as she answered.

"Put her on the phone!" he ordered. When Sasha handed her the phone, Angel looked surprised.

"Yes," she spoke softly at first, not knowing what to expect from the other end.

"I understand you know our friend, Mr. Castro." Stash was feeling her out, fishing for info.

"We have encountered each other in the recent past," Angel responded

"So what are you seeking out of him in this operation?"

"I don't think that's any of your concern, sir," she said boldly. "I have what you need and that's access to his home. Now I'm sure you guys are well equipped to bully your way in, but even that's not guaranteed to turn out well. Finesse has always been my Olsen method of operation. Believe me, I wasn't anticipating interference in my plan either, so I figured let's work together to see what we can get out of this mark." There was a long pregnant pause before he spoke.

"Okay, let's see how this plays out. Put Sasha back on the phone," he told her.

"Who?" Angel was confused. The person she was looking at was Shyanne or so she thought. The phone was handed to her with reservation.

"Yes, sir?"

"Continue on with the plan but work with this girl and see what she knows. It may benefit us."

Angel led them right to Castro's condo. Sasha realized someone had to be the bigger woman, so she lowered her ego and swallowed her pride, allowing Angel to take the lead. Besides, she was right. Finesse beats bullying when it comes to this kind of work. Angel noticed Sasha submitting to her, but she didn't relish in her position. They had a long night ahead and from the way things looked, they would need each other.

Castro had no clue the party would be ending at his spot with him all hooded up, but he would soon find comfort in the familiar scent of his own home. Angel punched the code in, disarming the alarm. A couple beeps and a click and they were in. Two masked men pushed him forcefully, leading him upstairs. Angel looked around remembering her first visit there. It was her only visit, but everything appeared the same. If that was the case, then she recalled he had a safe in his bedroom where he kept his valuables.

The night they were together, she was on a mission to cop a few dollars, basically anything worth her time. Castro was so enamored with Angel's figure, he could hardly contain himself. When she dropped her bra and panties to the floor, he lost all his faculties. She was so beautiful to him, and out of all the woman in the strip club, all the money he spent on the dancers, how was it that he took home the prize.

Angel sexed him like he was the last man on earth. Their night of hot, passionate lovemaking ended with Castro staggering off in a drunken stupor. Thinking he had put the mojo on Angel and rocked her to sleep, Castro carelessly went to the large tapestry that set above his dresser top. Pulling it back, he revealed a combination safe that kept attacks of money and other documents.

Not only was Angel awake but was conscious enough to make out the number sequence he used to gain access. It didn't benefit her then, but she felt one day it would come in handy. Castro thought he had an unforgettable one-night stand. He wasn't even concerned that she didn't give her name. To him, she was another conquered trophy to put on his shelf.

That night would prove to come back to haunt him. The circumstances were different, but her objective was set. Working him for anything she could get was the plan and if it meant working along side this crew, then so be it. She had nothing to lose, everything to gain. The people she was with seemed like professionals, very meticulous in their actions. And when she talked to Stash, she could tell he was their unspoken leader. So, instead of going against the grain, she decided to see how things would go.

"Damn, girl. Never thought you would do your boy like this!" Castro shot his angry words through muffled tones at her, the hood barely keeping him audible. "We had such chemistry."

"Sorry, Freddie. When I was in school, I didn't like chemistry much, so I switched subjects. I'm into math. This just adds up," Angel joked, kicking the man while he was down. There was a hint of seriousness in her tone. She knew from experience that he kept a nest egg in that safe. She just hoped nothing had changed from before.

"Angel, it's your move. We got him here. Now what do we do with him?" Sasha asked as she pointed to the hooded captive. Dozier had him detained pretty good where he couldn't wiggle. The mistake they made was not gagging his mouth.

"Oh, y'all two bitches think y'all got all the sense. Think y'all just gonna hit me up and get away with it?" He couldn't even get his statement out good before Dozier gave him a short jab to his side. The kidney shot took his breath away. "Shut up and do as they say," the normally silent, Dozier ordered.

"Bring him up here," Angel called from his bedroom. She stood in front of the faux Picasso that doubled as the hiding place for his safe. They brought Castro inside, sitting him in a chair at the foot of his bed. Dozier removed the black cloak covering his head, his eyes squinted at the sudden burst of light. After his pupils readjusted, he realized where he was at and instantly became angered.

By this time, Angel had the safe exposed, ready to work the combination. "Let me see if I remember correctly." Angel peeked over her shoulder, giving Castro a wink and a smile. She went to the keypad and confidently punched in the code she recalled seeing when she laid in his bed. It was wrong. She tried again unsuccessfully, Castro letting out a light chuckle.

"Did you actually think I would expose my hand to you, sweet Angel? I knew you weren't sleep that night. You were faking sleep almost as good as you faked your orgasm," he roared at his own joke.

"Enough with the games. Let me have a crack at it," Numbers demanded as she eased Angel out of the way. "Do you mind?" she asked Angel as if she had a choice. Numbers glared at her before Angel reluctantly conceded. This brought an even broader smile on Castro's face. He was the only one who had the number sequence to get in. Any attempt would be futile. He couldn't believe what he was seeing as Numbers got started.

She was an expert at anything with a keypad. She had a ritual and methods that no one could figure out. In her mind, there wasn't a lock or combination that couldn't be broken into. She ran her fingers across the pad a couple times, punched in a couple wrong codes, then on the third try, there was a click. Castro's eyes got big and his heart got heavy. His palms got sweaty too and his jaw dropped. There was no way he thought, yet Numbers opened the hefty metal door revealing its contents.

"How—how did you do that? I told no one that code, not even my mother." Numbers winked at him. The first time she cracked a smile all day, then she nodded at Sasha. "There you go, girl. Do what you do."

"Okay, let's see what we have here." She took out stacks of bills, ten thousand a bundle, tossing one to Angel. "Thanks, good work."

"Wait a minute. That's all I get?" Sasha ignored her, focusing on the rest of the merchandise. After all of the money was emptied, there was a manila envelop in the back marked "jackpot". As she went to open it, Castro pleaded with her. "Please, you can have everything else. Just leave that alone."

"Hold on, big boy. Now that would be rude. Momma always told he to clean my plate, don't leave anything behind. This sure looks important. Let's have a look."

Inside were a series of diagrams, like blueprints to an office building. There were different floors outlined, elevators, rooms, alarm systems, helipads, all types of things were detailed. He was right—it was a jackpot, especially when she saw the red circled vault on one of the pages.

"What's in the vault, Freddie?" Sasha asked nicely at first. Castro didn't answer. She gave Dozier a look and he knew exactly what that meant. With his massive hands, he grabbed one of his fingers and bent it back past the flexibility point until he heard a crack. The bone broke easily with Dozier's strength, Castro howling out in pain.

"My God! What do you want from me?" he cried out.

"Answers. Now what's in the vault?" There was a silence that didn't suit Sasha, so she gave Dozier another look. He made a move towards Castro.

"Okay, okay! Jewels! Precious jewels," he panted out

"What kind of jewels? That could be anything. Be more specific."

"Diamond, emeralds, rubies, sapphires. That floor has the offices for some important import/export director and his associates.. They're Africans who travel back and forth from the Ivory Coast. They own the whole building, but it's only a cover for the riches that are on that floor."

"And where is the building?" He knew she was serious about inflicting pain, so he offered her the information.

"Potomac."

"Why there? There are plenty of office spaces in DC."

"Exactly," Numbers cut in. " No one would suspect such an elaborate operation out in the suburbs. Makes sense."

"I must warn you. They are heavily guarded, armies of soldiers inside, wild Africans not afraid to die. Plus high tech alarm systems, motion sensors, and the whole nine. That's why I never moved on it. It was a lost cause. A sure death."

"Well, now we will decide the next move."

Dozier hit him on one of his pressure points around his neck area, knocking him out cold. The crew left as quietly as they came, heading back to the safe house with the take for the night. Angel looked at Sasha before she pondered her long ride home.

"You want us to send a driver to drop you home or arrange an Uber?"

"Honestly, I really want to be part of the team," Angel replied, looking at the crew of loyal compatriots with envy.

"That I'll have to run by the boss. Right now, all I can offer is a lift."

"I'll take that."

Chapter 5: Next Man Up

"Does the defense have anything else to present?"

Stash and his lawyer conferred for a brief moment then the lawyer nodded before he spoke to the judge.

"No, sir, your honor."

"Okay, the prosecutor recommends a sentence of three years for the defendant. I'm going to accept her recommendation. I pray that your time in the federal penitentiary is fruitful. Learn from the errors of your ways, so you I'll be better fit for your return to society. Please take the defendant into custody."

The gavel slammed down with an eerie echoed that Stash will never forget. His crew sat in the back of the courtroom in utter silence, wondering what would be the fate of their leader. In the back of each of their minds, they wondered who would take over the reigns as the orchestrator. Jobs were still out there to be done and there was plenty of money in the streets unclaimed. The couldn't just put the business on hold while he was away. No, that's not how he intended for things to go.

Before he left through the heavy oak doors leaving the courtroom, Stash took one last look over his shoulder and caught the eyes of his faithful team, Sasha, in particular.

"Y'all know what to do. Hold it down until I touch the turf."

Some gave fist pumps, others gave Stash a thumbs up. Out of the eleven of them, only a select few would come and see him on visitation days. There's a certain loyalty between them, an honor among thieves so to speak. But deep down in his gut, he could already figure who would show and who wouldn't.

It was unfortunate how things turned out. Stash had been doing good staying off the radar. Its like they say, what's done in the dark will eventually come to the light. As much as he hated to admit it, his past has come back to haunt him. What started out as a simple night out at the club, turned into something way more extra, something he could've never predicted.

Stash never really enjoyed the club scene. He was more of a homebody. The potential of money always motivated him, so when an associate of his asked to meet at a club called Phenomenon, he agreed. His reluctance to be in the club showed in his body language as he strolled towards the bar area. His annoyance was even more evident when he got a text stating the meeting would be delayed. Stash hated folks to be late. He would always say that was the beginning of bad business.

After a couple Coronas at the bar, Stash decided to move around a bit. The music was intoxicating—a mixture of Reggae and hip-hop thumping through the club's sophisticated sound system. Finding a spot on the wall, he was able to survey the landscape. "An opportunist's wonderland,", he said to himself. Just not his cup of tea. Nightclubs make great money, but they have a short life span. Not to mention the costly overhead and the insurance was a monster within itself. All sorts of accidents seem to happen at clubs. Shootings, stabbings, fights, too much to risk in the course of any given night.

"Hey there, handsome," a soft voice broke through the raucous atmosphere and invaded his thoughts. He was shocked he even heard her over the noise. Whatever the case, her arrival was a pleasant surprise. He looked up, catching her hazel eyes and smiled. It was hard to get a reaction out of Stash. He was always very stoic, in control. She got it.

"Hello, yourself," he responded coolly. It didn't take long before the conversation took over the moment. He kept things cordial, never one reveal too much about himself or his business. Stash would never risk the integrity of his empire on a stranger. But to entertain a stranger, especially a beautiful one, didn't cost him nothing but time.

Stash looked down at his phone and saw two missed calls, one was from his contact. He excused himself to handle his business, but not before he bought her another drink. That was just the gentleman in him. When he returned from his call, he was taken aback by what he saw.

The woman he was just getting to know was being disrespected by a tall, lanky dude with a loud rust colored, satin outfit. He chuckled at first when he approached and heard the country island spewing from his mouth. The woman appeared to be very serious, matching his words with some choice words of her own. She saw Stash and her demeanor turned soft.

"Well, here's my man. Now, say what you gotta say to him," she barked out confidently, drawing the attention of on lookers.

Stash was totally thrown by her display. He didn't like how she threw him under the bus. "Your man?" he thought. He wondered when did that happen, before or after the drinks? The real question was, how were things gonna go from here?

"You ain't go nothing to do with this ol' square ass nigga!" he shouted loud enough for some passersby to look in their direction. Imagine that he had some nerve to call Stash square, wearing satin in the new millennium. One thing Stash didn't go for was dudes who showed out in the public for the benefit of a woman.

"You're absolutely right. I don't have anything to do with this," he said calmly, which allowed the guy to relax his posture. Stash took notice, then pounced on the opening. "But I'm putting myself in it."

As he spoke the words, he delivered a throat shot so vicious, the man started choking and gagging, struggling to catch his breath. Stash didn't give him a chance to recover striking him again to the nose. Instantly, it splattered blood, dripping down on his gaudy shirt. Blood mixed with rust made the shirt look like tie-dye, an ugly color coordination. He tried to speak but all he could do was spit blood.

The man's pride was hurt bad. He tried to salvage any signs of his reputation by taking a swing at Stash. It was telegraphed, like he saw it coming like yesterday. He easily avoided contact from the wild hook, then used his momentum to take his balance away. Calmly, Stash put the man in a hold that applied pressure to his arm, holding him there until security arrived.

Once the scene cleared, Stash excused himself from the bar, leaving the woman standing there wondering what went wrong between them. She had no clue how bad she'd violated him, taking him way out of character. With Stash, you can either be all the way on or all the way off. She turned him off by putting him on the spot like she did.

That whole incident was uncalled for and could've been avoided easily. Women tend to react with emotion rather than logic. So she shouldn't have been surprised when left her there without warning, no good bye or nothing. All he wanted to do was put that day behind him, forgetting it ever happened.

Little did he know he would have to answer to the actions that took place the night. The unforeseen happened to Stash while driving to the safe house about a year and a half after the incident at the club. On a routine traffic stop, the authorities ordered a search of his vehicle. After some back and forth, Stash conceded figuring he had nothing to worry about. His memory failed him that evening because what they found in the console caused him to be looked up.

He forgot to do something with the 17-clip cartridge that went to the 9mm pistol he had registered to the name Justin Willis. That was one of his aliases. Problem was he had already given him an identification with another name. Surely he couldn't produce a second ID revealing yet another identity. He just had to hope nothing came up on his name, which he was about 99% certain it wouldn't. It was that 1% he couldn't account for.

There was an outstanding warrant for his arrest by a gentleman named Brice Roundtree. The charge was assault with bodily harm. Stash couldn't recall anything recent happening. He barely left the comfort of his home. Then it dawned on him, the woman from the club and that lame nigga.

Did he really take out a warrant on me, he thought *After all this time?* Evidently he did, according to the officer of the law. He most certainly did and with the intent to make a serious case of it. What he didn't account for was the cop catching Stash slipping with weapon paraphernalia in his possession, making the situation that much worse.

Because the crime happened in Maryland, it automatically became a federal offense and a whole different ball game. Stash had to get things organized and fast. Part of that was finding good legal representation, then finding someone capable to head up the operation in his absence. Not too many qualified to actually lead his crew, especially in his line of business.

Greed, envy, and betrayal all play a part in the game they played. That element wasn't something he wanted to stir up within his squad. Whoever he chose had to be up for the challenge of bringing in the jobs that brought in the most money and be responsible enough to make sure everybody ate.

For several weeks, Stash slowly withdrew from his normal activities and just observed the team. He saw who was capable and who was just good at the position they were already playing. Surprisingly, it was the women who appeared to be natural leaders, especially one in particular. Sasha's ability to organize and carry it out to the end impressed Stash. She had a knack for details, which was a key asset. Would the others be jealous if she was thrust into leadership? No question about it. Would they respect her? Over time, especially if the business is handled correctly and more importantly fairly.

How she worked the situation with Freddie Castro spoke volumes. There were a lot of moving parts and unexpected variables that could've made that whole night go left. But she was able to make things happen, smoothed out the bumps in the road and delivered a happy ending. She was the Messiah that night, turning water into wine. There's still a much bigger job to table. Pulling it off will take the skills and expertise of every member of the team. If not coached right, there could be casualties, ones they don't need.

Stash pretty much made his choice and he had a good feeling about it. His inner voice kept asking, would they respect her once he was behind the walls? He didn't see any reason why they shouldn't besides maybe jealousy, which was a common divider. He was willing to roll the dice.

As the verdict was being read, all he could think about was keeping things afloat for the three years he would be incarcerated. He knew with solid legal representation, he could get that number down. Legal representation, something else Sasha prearranged without having to be prepped, asked or guided to do. That was just one more check in the box marked "Ride or Die Bitch".

Leaving the courtroom, accompanied by the bailiff, he managed a smile and a thumbs up knowing all was in good hands. The crew thought the thumbs up was for them as a collective. Partially yes, but their new leader knew who was now in charge.

The End...